'A moody, modi[...]
need to make [...]
meditation on ce[...]

'An escapologist plans to replicate a death-defying feat that even the great Houdini abandoned as too dangerous; a news photographer assembles a macabre portfolio from the crime scenes of a serial killer; the police interrogate a suspect over the murders; a showbiz old-timer recounts his days on stage and screen; as the curtain-raiser to a beauty contest, an illusionist's assistant is locked into a sword cabinet for a final, dramatic performance: these are the finely spun threads that Edric weaves into a compelling whole. Their link is Mitchell (the closest we get to a central character), an embezzler and failed entertainment impresario on the point of his last, desperate stage act. It is his tale – the search for the truth of his mother's past – that provides the novel's focus.

Once the novel has you in its various grips it doesn't let go . . . Edric's skills are displayed on every page, in prose that manages to be at once spare and lyrical . . . It is a kaleidoscope of a book: its patterns tantalise at first, then clarify; then, just as we think we are making sense of them, they disintegrate and re-form into something new and even more dazzlingly brilliant'

MARTYN BEDFORD, *LITERARY REVIEW*

'The novel's fascination lies in the contrast between its noisy fragmented surface and the quiet exploration of human nature underneath'

FRANK EGERTON, *FINANCIAL TIMES*

'Theatrical illusion is his main theme, and each story approaches it differently . . . its subject matter can't fail: show business, seasides and crime. These were magical ingredients in fiction from Goethe's *Wilhelm Meister* to Graham Greene's *Brighton Rock*, and they've rarely let a novelist down since'

RUTH SCURR, *THE TIMES*

'Explores the faded territory of failing impresarios, seedy glamour and illusions which, while sustaining humdrum lives lived out on stage or screen, are also capable of rending them to dust . . . Edric neatly collates these fragments from the world of bedrock mid-century entertainment into a series of puzzles . . . the sleight-of-hand and the gnomic glances give his books their sheen: the occasional prompt sign would be ruination. Unlike Mitchell's diffident fumblings with his retractable knives, *The Sword Cabinet* is a thoroughly arresting performance'

D.J. TAYLOR, *SUNDAY TIMES*

'Mitchell, like some clod-hopping Alice, hot-foots through Wonderland reluctantly adoring the powdery façades, the scandalous illusions, while stumbling upon serial killings, debt, failure and an ex-mermaid (whom he marries). Edric's gloriously discomforting and mysterious novel . . . is a philosophical puzzle as to how, and if, it is possible to disentangle a life from its socially failed, yet genetically proud, inheritance'

ALISON HUNTLEY, *INDEPENDENT*

Robert Edric's previous novels include *Winter Garden* (1985 James Tait Black Prize winner), *A New Ice Age* (1986 runner-up for the Guardian Fiction Prize), *A Lunar Eclipse* (1989), *The Earth Made of Glass* (1994), *Elysium* (1995) and *In Desolate Heaven* (1997; also published by Anchor). He lives in East Yorkshire.

THE SWORD CABINET

Robert Edric

TRANSWORLD PUBLISHERS LTD
61–63 Uxbridge Road, London W5 5SA
A division of The Random House Group Ltd

RANDOM HOUSE AUSTRALIA (PTY) LTD
20 Alfred Street, Milsons Point, NSW 2061, Australia

RANDOM HOUSE NEW ZEALAND LTD
18 Poland Road, Glenfield, Auckland, New Zealand

RANDOM HOUSE (PTY) LTD
Endulini, 5a Jubilee Road, Parktown 2193, South Africa

This paperback edition published 2000 by Anchor, a division of Transworld
Publishers

First published in Great Britain by Anchor, 1999

10 9 8 7 6 5 4 3 2 1

Copyright © 1999 by Robert Edric

A catalogue record for this book is available from the British Library

ISBN 1862 30066 6

Typeset in 11½/16pt Adobe Caslon by Kestrel Data, Exeter

Printed in Great Britain by Mackays of Chatham plc, Chatham, Kent

For
Aaron and Ellie
&
Rachel and Jenny

1

Like every other confused and sorry tale that sets out to explain more than it can ever hope to, this one, Mitchell's confused and sorry tale, ended badly because it began badly, because it began – just as it begins again here – all too literally in glimpses and shadows, whispers and echoes, clouded memories and tales repeated second-hand, tales born of nothing solid, nothing tangible – nothing Mitchell might have pointed to and said, 'Look, here, at last, evidence, proof, a connection, something verifiable, confirmation, something indisputable, here, look, this is why I am what I am.' A place of shifting allegiances, new names, new coats of paint, mis-understandings and new understandings. It was Show Business – it was the unreliable yet necessary difference between what you saw and what you got; false starts, deceptive appearances and trick endings. It ended badly because nothing was ever what it seemed in that world: day might have been night; a nightmare – a dream; good luck – bad luck; expectation – despair; and the golden glow of a bright new dawn was all too often the glimmer of a fire in which someone stood screaming, unheard, to be saved.

And it also ended badly because it began in the tangle of speculation and inconsistency out of which nothing firm and incontrovertible ever grew; and because, finally – *finally* – at the age of forty-one – Mitchell's age when he discovered all of this – his father had died in un-suspecting seconds of a cerebral haemorrhage that flooded his brain and killed him somewhere between the beginning and the end of an unheard breakfast sentence, leaving him alone and face down in a plate of tepid food, with egg on his face and a thin course of blood running from his ear into the corner of his mouth, and looking in the photograph Mitchell was eventually shown as though someone had carefully drawn a line connecting the two points, giving his father the appearance of a ventriloquist's dummy. The poetic justice of this was not lost on Mitchell.

There had been nothing between the two men for eighteen years, and Mitchell hadn't seen him for twelve years before he died. There was no-one else. The man had been the last pale, spindly tree to fall in that particular part of the blighted forest.

Everything came to Mitchell. A house, which he quickly sold, and which was afterwards just as quickly demolished to make way for a new road; and countless pieces of drab furniture already thirty years out of date when Mitchell was a boy.

The money from all this was lost over the next few years in one failed venture after another, culminating in the club which Mitchell had now managed for two years, and where he lived with Laura.

No-one else had turned up at the funeral. The solicitor had seemed surprised that even Mitchell remained. There was no will, and Mitchell might just as easily not have been found — except, of course, for those threadbare ties which remained for ever in place and which bound together all slowly disintegrating families, however dismissive or unsuspecting of each other, through all the slow unravellings and cold evaporations of time and distance.

Sit next to somebody talking about having had fleas, Mitchell once said, and you soon start itching. Sit thinking about somebody who knew all about that sudden bloody explosion and God alone knows what you were going to start believing.

2

Clarence King's final flight lasted only four seconds, and somewhere along his low and misaligned trajectory, at a point approaching its unexpected zenith, the 'Cut-Price Cannonball' suffered what the coroner afterwards referred to as a 'not wholly unexpected and massive heart attack', and died. The other Kings at the inquest rose in uproar at this and the proceedings were delayed as several of them were removed. When the coroner resumed he said there was nothing more to add.

In the poorly focused and juddering film of the flight, Clarence emerges from the tapering mouth of the cannon through a rolling fist of smoke. He is an unrecognizable shape, his legs together, arms pressed tightly to his sides. And then he brings his arms forward, pointing ahead of him, a swimmer diving into his sea of blue sky over the water below. Frame by frame, this action can be seen, making a man of the projectile, but in the running film it is barely noticeable.

There was no real aerodynamic benefit to Clarence in having his arms cleaving the air ahead of him, but it was what the watching crowd expected, and it did at least create the semblance of a man in control of his own curving path towards the far shore and waiting net.

The water below him was the River Medway. It had been Clarence's ambition to be fired over every estuarine river wide enough – narrow enough, that is – to be spanned with the machinery and explosives then available. The year was 1946.

And just as the indeterminate missile became a man, and thereby something worth watching, so the following cloud of smoke also metamorphosed from a fist into a giant ring, dark against the pale sky, well defined and endlessly turning in on itself along its own much slower trajectory until long after Clarence had returned to earth. The ring, of course – the laws of aerodynamics again being slavishly obeyed – rather than follow Clarence along his own fatal path, continued upwards from the mouth of the cannon in a gentle arc into the warm air, upward into a flight of gulls, panicked by the explosion, before the cameraman who was following it realized what was happening – what, in the way of most amateur cameramen, he was *missing* – and then turned his machine back to where Clarence was supposed to have been, but wasn't, catching him instead at possibly the instant of his death, when his hitherto graceful ascent was broken by the folding of his legs and by one of his arms dropping from the other. There was still sufficient momentum to push the body along its intended course, but the limbs out of alignment, followed by the lazy turn of Clarence as a whole, acted as an effective brake and started his descent.

Between the rising ring of smoke and the mouth of the cannon there can also be seen the wooden platform upon which Clarence had waited inside the cylinder, and which acted as the protective base of his projectile body as it was forced upwards along the smooth bore of the cannon.

It was this wooden plug, Mitchell was later told, which was the key to any firing, and which created the impressive circle of smoke that followed Clarence out.

In the film, the small wooden platform falls spinning to earth like a giant tossed coin. It was the job of one of the younger, apprentice Kings to watch this closely and then to run and retrieve it.

There was some speculation at the inquest that Clarence might have died at the moment of the explosion beneath his feet, but the film clearly shows him raising his arms and completing the first few seconds of his ascent as expected.

Clarence would not have been facing forward when he died. His helmeted head would have been down. If he saw anything in those fatal seconds, then it was the water beneath him, dazzling and calm in the slack turn of the late-afternoon tide.

Equally likely is that he died in total silence. His padded helmet was designed to cover his ears, to come low over his brow and to cup the base of his skull. Its double straps were fastened beneath and across his chin, protecting his jaw by keeping it firmly clamped. He would also have been biting hard on a gumshield.

On other occasions he had worn goggles, but he complained that these caused his temples to bleed. Much more common were the nosebleeds he suffered, although these, strangely, seldom occurred during the flight itself, coming instead hours afterwards when he was asleep and spreading unstanched over his pillow and sheets.

The giant net uselessly awaited him on the western shore, perfectly tensed and angled and strung between its swaying poles, and with its own smaller crowd shielding their eyes against the glare out of which Clarence was supposed to come.

The Cut-Price Cannonball – Clarence's billing since only the previous year – did not fall into the Medway, but came down instead into an area more mud than water and in which were studded the countless wooden piles of abandoned jetties. At the inquest, reference was made to his left foot, severely injured, post-mortem, by collision with an iron bolt protruding from one of these piles.

It had been Clarence's idea to be fired across the rivers rather than merely through space. The distances were more or less the same, and the aerodynamic limits of the flights no more or less difficult to calculate. But the rivers provided a second, more spectacular achievement – an obstacle to be overcome rather than merely a target to be struck.

Watching the film, and knowing that the cameraman is not seeing what he is recording – or, if he is seeing it, then not fully understanding what he is seeing – it is a simple enough task to pick out the precise moment of Clarence's death, that exact point where the X line of living bisects the Y line of death, and where the curve starts all too literally to follow one course and not the other. It is there most forcibly in the sag of Clarence's first dropped arm. His flexed or folded leg might have been an involuntary movement – the way a spasm might suddenly bend a standing man – but the dropped arm destroying the arrow of his flight was much more than an unavoidable reflex. That dropped arm marks the point at which a third line enters the graph, a line wavering above and below the gentle curve of imminent death, a line at which another death – the death of showmanship – occurs, where every urge or impulse to maintain the outward appearance of a planned performance is finally overridden. The gathered Kings understood this, even if the coroner did not.

Until Morgan's death, eight years later, Mitchell could not imagine a more fitting death for a King.

Everyone had believed Clarence to be in his early thirties, but at the inquest it was discovered that he was thirty-nine. And again, this came as no real surprise to the true Kings.

If it was not planned, then Clarence's fall seemed, perversely, as graceful as his ascent. Had his heart not imploded until a second later, then who is to say that he might not have followed his projected course and landed in the net? Who is to say that his landing would not have been drowned in applause and not the breath-held vacuum of silence and unblinking disbelief which instead followed him down to the mud? He was not some shot bird turning instantly from grace and energy into disarray, but a man who had died, as every man must, whether out in the open or hidden away, in a warm and blinding moment where the suspension of disbelief and the frailty of existence had briefly touched and thrown off their sparks.

Clarence's Cut-Price value referred to the fact that the spectacle of his flight was free of charge, while the sideshows and stalls of the numerous other, less daring Kings made the money of the day. The name, like Morgan's title later, was turned instantly into cheap headlines, and after that cheap jokes.

He was a man. He was fired from a cannon. He died when his heart died. And dead, his corpse fell into a cushion of mud while his wreath of fading smoke rose slowly over him.

3

In the eyes of the Kings, Quinn, despite his ancestry, had long since ceased to exist. Denouncing the name had condemned him to oblivion.

At the time of Morgan King's death, Quinn was Mitchell's mother's legal guardian. Mitchell's mother was Morgan's girl assistant. Quinn was the last of the true Kings, the last of the showmen.

He had refused to attend the wedding of Mitchell's parents. He had warned her against marrying the man. Mitchell's father would have nothing to do with the Kings or the shabby-exotic world they inhabited, and all Mitchell had ever known of Quinn as a boy had been what he remembered his mother telling him before her own slow tumble into premature senility and the powdery collapse of the past.

It was she who had told him that Quinn had worked with Morgan in America, first in travelling shows and then in the film industry. He was never a billed or contracted actor, at best an extra, another lost face in the scenes of lost epics; or perhaps he was a carpenter, or an electrician, or a man carrying a chandelier, a Roman shield or a tray of custard pies from one set to another.

And, as elsewhere in Mitchell's search, all these once-firm lines of connection turned inevitably to dashes and then to dots and then to nothing, blank spaces in which he alone was left to wander.

His mother had lost contact with Quinn after her marriage. Much later, beyond all possibility of reconciliation, she had expressed the wish that Mitchell had known the man, that he had still been a presence in their lives.

And now Mitchell wanted to know what Quinn knew of his mother, and of Morgan, in the weeks and months prior to Morgan's own bloody and spectacular farewell appearance before the audience of the world.

He spent ten months, on and off, searching, told by all the minor Kings he managed to trace that Quinn was long since dead.

But Quinn, it transpired, was not dead. Nor was he dying. And nor, despite his age – Mitchell calculated this at somewhere between eighty-nine and ninety-three – had the frost of senility gained anything but the most tenuous of holds on him.

Quinn remembered everything. He would not, he insisted, tell Mitchell all of it, but he remembered it. And unlike most of the other older Kings Mitchell had already encountered, Quinn did not retreat willingly into the past. He did not forever make the comparisons which cast their shadows over the present and the future. To Quinn, unlike those others, the past was neither that golden glow nor warming blaze. To Quinn, it was the cold wreckage of that blaze in which the man screaming to be rescued had long since fallen silent.

Upon finally meeting him, Mitchell saw immediately how Quinn must have been as a young man. He saw too what Quinn had been to his mother, and why he and Mitchell's father had been openly and enduringly hostile towards each other. He remembered that his mother spoke of Quinn almost as though they had been lovers. He calculated that thirty-three years had separated them.

The first thing Mitchell told Quinn upon finally meeting him was that he would have travelled to America to see him if necessary.

'Then sound more convincing when you say it,' Quinn said.

He lived in a ground-floor flat in a house in Battersea, reached along a high, narrow passage leading from the front door. There had once been panels of coloured glass in the door, but these were now lost and boarded over. A dozen flimsy buttons and nameplates, some dimly illuminated, some with their slender wires exposed, lined the wall beside the door. A dozen plastic bins stood in what had once been a small garden, but which was now concreted over, and where a struggling hydrangea grew through the concrete as though in remembrance of what lay buried beneath.

Mitchell pressed the bell and stood closer to the door to listen. He expected to hear nothing, for there to be a long delay, for Quinn to come cautiously and suspiciously to let him in. But instead the old man came to the door immediately, holding a folded newspaper and several envelopes which he had just then gathered up from the floor. He beckoned Mitchell in. It was much cooler in the hallway than outside. Gas and electricity meters lined one wall. The pattern of small tiles on the floor was disintegrating, and loose pieces lay along the skirting like a long-abandoned puzzle.

Quinn indicated his door. His one distinguishing feature – distinguishing him as a King, that is – was the single gold earring he still wore, partly obscured in the dusk of the passage, and hidden too by the way the lobe of his ear was pressed flat against the skin of his neck. Quinn had once performed as a strongman, and it was how, despite his age, he now looked to Mitchell.

His flat consisted of a sitting room with a window looking out on to the patch of cement, a bedroom and a kitchen. He told Mitchell he shared a bathroom on the first landing. Bookcases lined one wall and Mitchell surreptitiously searched these for the signs he had seen elsewhere: magazines, old posters, framed advertisements, plastic-wrapped costumes still hanging behind doors, silver shoes, packed cases and locked diaries like those left to him by his mother, and which had brought him here today.

Quinn saw him doing this. 'They're not here,' he said. 'Flotsam and jetsam. You'll have seen enough of that already.'

Mitchell asked him if any of his own generation of Kings was still alive. He knew that Quinn had been one of four brothers, one of whom had drowned crossing a canal in Holland during the war. It had been the Kings' only known wartime casualty, and Mitchell's mother had told him the story often. She had been a girl of six when the war had ended, was living then with Quinn, and the death of his youngest brother had bound them more tightly together. A photograph of the dead boy stood on one of the bookcases, and Mitchell was relieved at seeing it there, confirmation, a connection. Then Quinn asked him if he wanted to see pictures of his mother as a girl and young woman, but when he said he did, Quinn said, 'Later.'

Mitchell could only guess at the depth of the hurt Quinn must have felt when his mother abandoned him for his father. Guess, too, at the weight of her own regret ever after.

Quinn fetched a tray from the kitchen. It had been prepared in readiness for Mitchell's visit.

It was the end of July and there had been no rain for six weeks. For a fortnight the sun had risen and fallen in cloudless skies. The small room in which they sat – this spartan set with its props and players – felt airless.

'You want to know about Morgan,' Quinn said.

'And the others. And my mother.'

'But Morgan most of all, eh? "Ice Man" Morgan. Salvation of the Kings, destroyer of the Kings.'

'Did you know him well?'

'Well enough not to stop him from doing what he did.'

'Did anyone try?'

'The Kings? It was the kind of thing they lived for. Oh no, they were all encouragement and applause from the word go. Not one of them prepared to take his place, of course, but making all the noise and blowing all the hot air he needed to stick himself at their centre and get on with things.'

'How did my mother become his assistant?'

'By default. Morgan had a daughter of his own, but unknown to him, unknown to anybody, unknown probably even to herself then, she was pregnant. Another one of the Kings' miraculous conceptions. It took Morgan at least six months of preparation to set up the illusion the way he wanted it. I fastened his chains, I bound him in his ropes, I tied up his sacks and locked him in his airtight trunks and coffins.'

'Did you work with him on his last act?'

Quinn shook his head. 'Your mother was already with me. She'd come to me two years earlier. There was no-one else to take her. She was a fast learner. It was what she wanted, then. Morgan took a liking to her. She was mostly decorative, assistant in name only. They found her a costume and it fitted.'

'Did she have any choice?'

'I doubt it. She was keen to do it. There were plenty of others ready to take it on. He was, after all, Morgan, remember, undisputed King of Kings. As I say, he took a liking to her. It was how things worked, how things got done.'

'Do you think *he* had any serious doubts about what he was doing?'

'Did she tell you anything at all?'

'She refused point-blank. After Morgan, after that night, she had nothing more to do with any of them.'

'Me included,' Quinn said. 'And she'll have told you she was eighteen when it happened, nearly nineteen. She wasn't. She was barely fifteen. She might have passed for eighteen, but she wasn't. It was part of her appeal for Morgan. He liked them young. And you have to remember that all this was less than two years after he'd been arrested on suspicion of murder.'

'And cleared of all charges. They caught the man who did it.'

'Did they? It still left its mark on him, tainted them – us – all. There were plenty who believed him guilty at the time.'

'Even among the Kings?'

'Especially among the Kings. They knew him better than anyone.'

Mitchell had not been prepared for this. It was what, two years before his spectacular finale, had first brought Morgan to prominence. It was why people remembered his name. It was why the events of two years later had caused such a sensation.

'You should have come to her funeral,' Mitchell said eventually.

'Cremation.' Quinn recited the date, time and place. 'Why?'

'I would have appreciated meeting you then.'

'I doubt it. And none of the others would. Did many of them turn out for her?'

'None,' Mitchell said.

'They went off funerals.'

The front door opened, banged shut and someone passed along the passage and climbed the stairs. Another door and then footsteps crossed the room above them. A television was switched on, its muted voices and laughter coming down to them through the ceiling.

Quinn looked up at it. 'We'll laugh at anything,' he said.

'These days?' Mitchell added, immediately regretting the remark.

Quinn passed him a cup and saucer and then took his own.

'Anything,' Quinn repeated, and then, unexpectedly, turning to face Mitchell, said, 'I was the voice of the donkey. You probably don't even remember the advert. Commercial. Cinema-release only. One of the first. Must have been. Remember it? You probably never even saw it. Of course you didn't see it. You weren't even born.'

And again, before Mitchell could grasp it, history disintegrated and then reformed to tell another story, another story completely, and just like the disintegrating pattern of tiles in the hallway, the centre was lost and the scattered edges held the only clues to the vanished picture he was there to assemble.

4

Another, earlier beginning. This. This photograph: not a particularly clear photograph, black-and-white, and with definition faded further by the passage of time and the cheap paper on which it was printed. Not a photograph a professional news photographer of today might be proud to have taken, but at least it establishes another time and place, the third of Mitchell's cardinal points. And a photograph which gave full play to the imagination of whoever looked at it.

It is the photograph shown to Morgan on the second day of his questioning.

It may be a deceit of the present age or of human nature in general to believe we see what others have seen before us, but in some instances it is a deceit worth building upon: the police station still exists, the layout and the function of most of its rooms remains the same, the cells are still the cells down in the cellar.

They might, for instance – that person looking at the photograph for the first time – want to imagine the remainder of the woman's body, to guess at her figure, her age, her face, the colour of her hair, the make-up and perfume she may or may not be wearing. They might want to imagine how her hands are held, whether her fingers are bunched into fists, or splayed; whether her hands are held together or apart; whether or not they are tied – did they carry the marks of having been bound? – or are they frozen in the clutch from which her murderer pulled himself free? Are her nails painted – nails beneath which clues may yet linger? Is she wearing any rings? All of those things.

She was said to have been engaged to be married. She was also said – opening up the picture to even further speculation – to have had 'several' (some reports said 'many') men-friends and male acquaintances, and to be well-known and liked ('popular') at the club, and others like it, which she was known to frequent, in which she spent her last night alive, and in which, according to a dozen eyewitnesses, some understandably more reliable than others considering the gloom and discreet lighting of the place, she met a man answering to Morgan's description, and with whom she was afterwards seen to leave at some time between one and one-thirty in the morning.

She was blonde because the description of her in the accompanying article said she was blonde, though whether natural or dyed remains a guess; whether honey- or straw- or platinum- a surmise. It is not a difficult game to play for anyone possessed of that common enough mix of prejudice and intuition. What kind of woman is murdered as she was murdered? What kind of woman spends her nights in those clubs with those men and then brings them afterwards to places like this?

Morgan never denied that he had been in the club, nor that he had spoken to the woman and had bought her a drink. He said he recalled that they left at the same time, though not 'together' in the way the police were using the word.

He wants to know who might have seen the two of them together after leaving the club, but no-one tells him.

Another sudden, chemical flash in which the small room – now the Scene Of The Crime – dissolves and then slowly re-forms, re-emerges, and everything is fixed. Voices are silenced, men crowded together pause in their actions. Some might even consider that here was a woman alive and laughing only twelve or fourteen hours earlier.

A distant siren, perhaps, another police car or the approaching ambulance, not the whooping electronic melody of today, more the sound of a bell being rung by hand, creating its own more specific sense of urgency and alarm. And beyond that? The rustle of mid-morning traffic in that part of south London, the whispering of the other tenants, the imagined echo of her own choked screams?

Why, they wanted to know, did he possess the woman's headscarf, a square of translucent near-silver? Because she had dropped it from the pocket of her coat and he had picked it up, intending to give it back to her. Give it back to her when? Later. He must have known her better than he had implied. The next time they asked him the question, he said he had also considered taking the scarf back down the steps of the club and leaving it at the cloakroom, where an attendant – one of the reliable witnesses – would have taken care of it.

Ah, but you didn't, did you? You kept it.

Morgan acknowledged the fact.

What was it? they asked him. A token, a souvenir, a memento?

None of those things, he told them.

But by then they were coming to know him, who he was, how he lived, the life he led. His name, you might say, was ringing bells. They were coming to know him, and they were beginning to savour what they knew.

5

Mitchell stood at the window of the flat he shared with Laura. He looked down and saw her as she came out of the club's fire exit and crossed the car park in the falling darkness below. She climbed the steps to the sea wall. He had often watched her, standing there, looking out over the void of the winter sea as though it were the edge of the world. She stood illuminated by the strings of lights which swayed above her. He knew she was aware that something was about to happen – that the train of events he had set in motion all those months ago was now heading swiftly to its conclusion, but she had not yet confronted him with her understanding of what that conclusion might be.

If she turned her back to the sea and looked across to

the club she would have been unable to avoid seeing him there, standing close to the glass and looking down at her.

It was New Year's Eve. A big night in the otherwise empty winter calendar of the failing club, a tradition, an occasion Mitchell had inherited with the lease of the place, and something over which he now had little control.

Believing that Laura had turned to look up at him, he half raised his arm to her, but she gave no indication of having seen him. He looked beyond her to the blink of distant lights, boats perhaps, to the scattered embers of other towns further along the coast, and to the sweeping beam of the town's lighthouse. Beyond all this, and looking back at him through the night, he saw only his own puzzled reflection, wide as the invisible horizon, built of flame and framed by the darkness which surrounded him.

6

Morgan's greatest and final illusion was to be frozen alive into a giant block of ice, chained and padlocked and bound with rope, from which, after a decent and death-defying interval, he would then burst free, the last Prometheus, cheered and applauded, risen in adulation, parading back and forth, his arms high, chest out, stamping the icy chill from his bones, with the last of the unwound chains and ropes dangling from his wrists. A fanfare of trumpets, preceded by a slow, steady heartbeat on the kettledrums as he prepared himself for his impossible resurrection and then crashed out into the disbelieving world.

That was Morgan's plan. And like Frankenstein and his monster before him, Life itself was to be the illusion.

It was a project he had harboured ever since learning of Harry Houdini's own abandoned preparations for making the attempt. He had been told in great secrecy about the rejected ice cabinet by a dealer in theatrical memorabilia who traded from a small shop in Cecil Court. The man had dealt with various others of the Kings in the past, acquiring their collections and paraphernalia as the last of the showmen and performers died. Morgan, many later suggested, had agreed to act as an agent for the dealer, acquiring the artefacts and mementoes at a greatly increased profit to them both.

Upon his return from America, Morgan moved with the Kings from the variety and music halls – dying worlds anyway – into the travelling fairs and circuses and end-of-pier shows. He dwelt on what he had been and he buried his failures in America beneath his vision of the greatness yet to come.

It was upon learning of Houdini's cancelled preparations that he began his own calculations.

Houdini had been sufficiently serious about the attempt to employ a small company of carpenters and glaziers, and even a metallurgist and a physicist from New York State University, to help him prepare the ice cabinet and the various means whereby the illusion might be achieved. Every conceivable need and eventuality had been calculated and woven into the changing designs and preparations, everything endlessly tested, every tiny theoretical part of the illusion examined again and again and again.

These preparations, which Morgan had known about for at least a decade prior to his own attempt in 1954, cost Houdini and his craftsmen and professors fifteen wasted months and a reputed $12,000, but at the end of that time there still remained too much uncertainty, too many intangibles, and so the project was abandoned.

Uncharacteristically – perhaps because he wanted to leave behind no evidence of his failure – Houdini never patented any of his designs for the cabinet and its working parts – a notable omission considering the extent and variety of his countless other patents, few as impressive overall as the cabinet, and some as simple and as seemingly inconsequential as the dimensions of a nail or a screw.

7 _____

'How many are we expecting for our big night?'

Her voice startled him. He saw her reflection in the glass, her head on his shoulders.

'Big night,' Mitchell said, his own dead tone matching hers. 'Who knows.'

'The very last Beauty Show. Think anyone's ever going to miss it?'

'Some of them. Not many. It's been going eight years. Knowing this place, it probably qualifies for a grant from the Heritage Commission by now.'

'We ought to be downstairs,' she said. 'The staff are arriving. The lights still need setting.'

They went down together. The stairs led backstage and to the dressing rooms. A door opened into the concert hall.

Mitchell went out on to the low stage. Lights flashed down at him and he called out for the man operating them to turn them off.

Laura waited at the side of the empty stage. She had been a singer, a dancer, half of an unfunny comic double act, and now this, magician's assistant to Mitchell, gatherer-in of doves, displayer of giant playing cards, a woman outlined in knives, sawed in half, pierced by swords, a woman ten years too old for the costumes she still wore.

The tragedy of her own life, she now understood, was that not only was it beyond her to leave him, but that it was also beyond her to prevent him from going. And after that, when he finally did go, it would be beyond her to follow him.

Mitchell shouted down to an imaginary audience. She watched him closely. Lights flickered into life at the far end of the cavernous room. Grilles were rattled and lifted on the three bars.

It was four o'clock, death of a winter's day, another three hours until the club opened. Before then, tables and chairs had to be set out, floors swept, musicians dealt with, the stage lighting fixed, bars stocked and the kitchen warmed into life. The beauty-show contestants would be there by six.

'Same band as last year?' she called to him. Her voice echoed in the high room, the words coming back to her in a whisper, something turned regrettable and secretive.

Out on the stage, Mitchell shrugged, affecting non-chalance. 'Probably,' he said.

Arrangements for the night had been set in motion four months earlier, at the end of the summer season. Last year, Mitchell had undertaken them all; this year others were involved: the town's Tourism and Recreation Committee, various councillors, the ad-hoc management team of a brand new leisure centre that might or might not be about to be built, and which existed already in a proudly displayed model in the foyer of the town hall.

Laura understood as well as Mitchell how quickly everything was now closing in on him. Financial irregularities. Mismanagement. Non-compliance. Mitchell cast his stones at bad luck, greedy creditors, uncaring and short-sighted officialdom, fickle audiences. Laura set her own sights more directly at the solid pillars of Fate and Consequence, stony ground and spilt seed.

They had gone separately to look at the model in its glass case, and although they had both seen beyond the developer's hoardings and had understood better than most the rough terrain between promise and fulfilment which lay there, they had each known exactly what they were witnessing and what they were now becoming an unwilling part of.

They had been together for five years. They had performed adult magic acts. Stag nights, private shows. Neither of them talked about the ending they faced together, but that was only because they both already understood it in all its necessary and varied details.

He ran the club on a lease from the town council. Hope had outreached ability; expectation had leap-frogged financial reality. Conditions had been imposed, percentages of investment and profit calculated. And he had failed. It was a common enough scenario in those years. The summer here was a different country, a different planet. Out of season the place was wrung dry. Some people survived, some didn't. Neither Mitchell nor Laura had lived in a seaside resort before, and neither of them had truly understood about that other country of winter.

'It's like living through another fucking ice age,' he had once said to her at the frozen heart of their first closed season.

8

'What made the police suspect Morgan in the first place?' It was something Mitchell had never discovered, but he knew it must have been more than the dead woman's headscarf.

'Cigars,' Quinn said. 'Havana cigars. Proper Cuban cigars. They had someone, some other out-of-work extra, come out wearing a Panama and a white suit. Black-and-white shoes. Pencil moustache, lip rouge, regular Clark Gable. He comes out holding this unlit cigar.' He paused and looked up at Mitchell. 'They arrested him because he was a suspect. He knew the woman. He'd been seen with her. She'd told someone about him. I don't know. Perhaps he just attracted too much attention to himself. Guy Somebody, that was the name of the man in the Panama. Or perhaps just guy, some guy.'

'They never seriously believed Morgan was responsible for all – what – four, five, killings, did they?'

Quinn was disappointed that his own tale had stalled and he did not disguise the fact from Mitchell.

'I doubt it. He was just a good suspect. Actor, theatrical, moving around, hand to mouth, eye for the ladies, ladies' man. Shine a light on some men and they fade away. Shine it on others and they double in size.'

'Did they talk to you about the killings?'

'Of course they did. Who knows, perhaps they even suspected *me*.'

'Of being his accomplice?'

'Of being the killer. I didn't always live in his shadow. I know it might have seemed like that to most people – that's how it looked to the rest of the Kings – but I did have my own life to lead.'

'Is that why you abandoned them all, why you left it all behind you?'

'Partly. Morgan was eleven years older than me. All my life they treated me as though I were his lucky son.'

It was not what Mitchell had expected. Morgan and Quinn had spent seven years together in America, long before Morgan's rise to prominence, the time of Quinn's forgotten commercial.

'Were you at his funeral?'

'We all were. The call went out. One big happy family. You could have rowed a boat on that pond of crocodile tears.'

'But you didn't stay with them afterwards?'

'Me and plenty of others.' Quinn rose from his chair and went into the adjoining bedroom. A dark wardrobe stood at the bottom of the bed, its top stacked with suitcases. He opened the wardrobe and took a shoebox from it. The sight of it, after so many others, disappointed Mitchell.

But Quinn came back to him holding only a single photograph. He sat back in his seat and looked closely at the picture. It occurred to Mitchell that there had been no searching involved, that this too had been sought out in advance of his visit. Quinn handed him the picture.

Mitchell angled it into the light of the window. A boy of nine or ten and a fat man sitting beside him. The boy looked puzzled, alarmed almost. The fat man wore a straw boater. He looked familiar. His chins hid his collar. Part of his hand was visible on the boy's shoulder. Light flared against both their foreheads. The man's eyes seemed too white, too well defined. The boy looked as though he was about to raise his hand to shield himself from the flash of the photographer's bulb.

'Thirteen,' Quinn said.

'The boy's you?'

'Don't tell me you haven't already seen it.'

Mitchell hadn't. Or if he had, then he hadn't remembered it.

'My claim to fame in those days.'

'Who's the man?' But even as he spoke, Mitchell put

a name to the face and said, 'Roscoe Arbuckle,' simultaneously with Quinn.

'You must have seen it.'

Mitchell remembered. 'One of the papers printed a picture of Arbuckle alongside one of Morgan after he'd been arrested.'

'The day before they released him.'

'Why?'

Quinn shrugged. 'Because that's what newspapers do.'

'Did they know you knew him, Arbuckle?'

'I doubt it. Perhaps I should have told them, got my own face in the papers.'

'It's what most of the other Kings would have done.'

'It's what they *all* would have done.'

'Did Morgan know him?'

' "Know" might be stretching a point. That picture, me and Arbuckle, that was the beginning and the end. Published in most of the trades, most of the locals, and I'm talking about Hollywood now, not here, there, Hollywood, America.'

'Was all this before or after Arbuckle's trial?'

'Before. A year or so. Perhaps not even that. Never forgot him. It was taken the day of his mother's funeral. That was the whole point of the picture, him with me. Didn't know me from the dirt on his shoe, but there I was. Looks like you could have fitted the whole of my head into his fat mouth.'

'Is there a picture of Morgan and Arbuckle, the two of *them* together?'

Quinn shook his head. 'Morgan never came close. They wanted a child to pose with him. A girl would have been better. I was skinny and poor and I looked it. Something in ringlets and a party dress would have suited them better.'

'But not afterwards?'

'No, not then.' Quinn took back the photograph. ' "Hey, señorita, got a light?" white-suit says, and then this Mex long-legger, a real mud-hut beauty, comes out from a doorway, all lit up under a street light and says to him, "You want a light, señor?" ' Quinn paused. ' "Hey, you wanna light, see-ñor?" Talking like she hasn't heard him, like she's still the all-to-live-for side of twenty-one, and shows him some more of that leg. And he says, "Sure I want a light." ' There was something now in the way Quinn spoke – not merely his exaggerated accent, but something more, something deeper – a natural and a cherished part of him which he could neither deny nor resist, and which warmed him as it rose to the surface. Mitchell had seen the same thing elsewhere – men and women waking from their dreams of the past and the better lives they lived there and still talking in the voices of those dreams. But with most of those others it had been contrived, done for effect, needing to impress; with Quinn, it seemed a genuinely uncontrollable and sustaining part of him, nourishing him as he spoke.

' "Sure I wanna light." By which time, see, the cigar-makers know they've got you watching. None of that was ever left to chance, not now, not then. Who wouldn't want a light from her, even if it was only to go on looking at what she had to offer? And it was all on view, believe me. Everything they could show us, we got to see. Long legs. Low-cut top.' He drew a line across his chest. 'So what that she can't count past a hand of fingers. So what that white-suit with his hat is poking her full of promises in his rented bungalow every night, so what?'

Mitchell detected the first dry note of regret. Quinn, too, saw that he had said too much, and stopped talking. He had been briefly mesmerized by the story he told, and this, too, Mitchell had seen elsewhere.

'You have to forgive my language,' Quinn said. 'You find things slipping in. Even after all this time.'

Mitchell acknowledged this small release of tension between them. 'What about the donkey?' he said.

'That's me. That's where I come in. "Hey, señorita, I got a light." But in the voice of a donkey. Big nose sound. "He-e-e-e-y, señori-i-i-i-ta." You get the idea. Awful idea, but you get it.'

Mitchell nodded.

'The animal comes on, all clipped and washed and wearing its own straw hat, its ears sticking up, taped at the back. "I got a light." So by now white-suit's looking surprised. A quick open mouth and gulp to camera. Sure, he's surprised. Talking donkey, right?'

'And the woman?'

'It's her donkey. Her donkey, my voice. Original idea was to have a donkey with an English accent. Somebody knows I'm working there, set-building, I get sent for. But it's another bad idea and it flops. Donkeys are meant to be stupid. So I give them my donkey voice and I'm in. Fifty dollars. The donkey spoke better than the woman. She only had six words to remember and they shot that twenty times over.'

'It's a good story,' Mitchell said, wondering where it was leading.

'It gets better. I got another twenty for making the noise of the donkey coming out of the shadow behind her, clip-clop clip-clop. That's me, too. Who else do you know who ever got famous for banging the two halves of a coconut together?'

9

'And can we have some calm, some quiet, some room to move. Please. Thank you.' He needs all those things to do his job properly. It is the man in charge at the scene of the crime, the senior detective, seeking promotion, wanting this to proceed exactly as it should proceed, as it is scripted in all the manuals to proceed. True to form, he wears a gabardine overcoat and a grey hat. A smoking cigarette, more in his hand than his mouth.

It is Thursday, the nineteenth of October, nineteen fifty-two.

And a dark suit with all its creases exactly where they should be, even if its pinstripe is not precisely met along its seams, even if the cuff of one sleeve is starting to fray. He holds up his hands, this man in charge, this man around whom everything must now revolve, to impress himself further on the men surrounding him.

The dead woman is still at his feet. Someone has draped a sheet from the bed over her head and the upper half of her body. Now only her legs remain revealed. The search for clues has yet to begin in earnest. The man in charge wants the world to stop for an hour and then for it to begin moving again with himself firmly in position.

Because of the nature and the scatter of the subsequent murders, there will soon be other men in charge, else-where, other little spiders working inwards on the same complicated web, in the same strong winds, at the centre of which, eventually, hopefully their prey will be caught.

'Quiet!' he shouts, and suddenly there is silence. Even the approaching siren no longer sounds, its echo fading in the empty streets behind it. He is uncertain what is required of him next. A woman has been murdered. Somewhere there exists her murderer. A line must be drawn. Though uncertain, he is comforted and reassured by the simple order he has already, and so easily, im-posed.

A voice calls out from the back of the room – first-floor landing, really, but the stage is set and the landing is included – asking if the sheet hiding the woman's head and body might be removed so that a better picture might be taken. The detective does not deign to answer, let alone comply.

And so the photographer, assuming he is even able to get close enough to take his precious picture, must be content with the two legs showing only from the knees down, the one scuffed white stiletto-heeled shoe on the carpet and the other hanging satisfyingly from her stockinged foot.

The room itself is little different from a hundred thousand others. A house of flats and bedsits, furnished, unfurnished, some lived in for the life of their tenants, others rented and vacated on a monthly basis; weekly, sometimes, when the need arises.

The landlady has already been seen. A witness who saw nothing of the crime, but who is only too willing to put the flesh of personality and character on the woman's dead bones. It has already been established that the population of the house is a transient one, more men than women, other women like the dead woman, and that the landlady will let rooms to anyone from labourers to theatrical people. She has a collection of framed, signed photographs from some of the latter and their names are noted. A labourer, however, might be deemed more likely to have possessed the strength required to kill the woman in the manner in which she was killed.

Already the language exists which allows no more to be given away than is absolutely necessary.

The detective in charge is also aware of the fact that the murderer himself – he is certain it is a man – might now be among the small group of other tenants gathered on the landing beside the photographer, looking in.

The room itself contains a wardrobe, mahogany-veneered but cheaply constructed, a dressing table, a paler wood, perhaps maple or oak, spread with the detritus of any lonely life: cosmetics, coins, several glasses, a half-bottle, half empty, of gin, cigarettes, used tickets, tissues, cheap jewellery, earrings mostly, but some rings and necklaces; and beside the dressing table a small bedside cabinet, gold and white wickerwork, from which a lamp has been knocked to the floor. Linoleum patterned to look like marquetry, but fooling no-one, and a carpet with a floral design – autumnal now – reaching to the foot of none of the four walls. An elongated diamond of mirror hangs on a chain from the picture rail. From this, the detective knows, he might calculate the height of the woman. Has the chain been recently adjusted? Have any fingerprints been left around the mirror's scalloped edges? Where in the room would he have to stand or sit to look into it and see the body on the floor? He opens and closes the wardrobe door several times. It may tell him something, but he is uncertain what. Lives, he knows, ordinary lives, are boxed up and stored away in wardrobes, and on top of them, and beneath them.

The window looks out over the street to the line of houses opposite. Other detectives will soon be knocking on the doors there. He will need to know if the bedside lamp was switched on or off before it was knocked to the floor and its bulb smashed. Is all the glass accounted for? Is it only in the crime stories he reads that a sliver of the bulb lies waiting in the turn-up of a man's trousers ready to point him to the noose? He indicates the lamp to one of his subordinates.

Nondescript bed and bedclothes, the usual mulch of dust and hair and screwed-up pieces of paper beneath. Curtains and nets both seen better days. Window that might not have been washed since the war. He will need to talk again to the landlady, allow her to lead him through and around her pathetic domain.

'Just one shot,' the photographer persists. 'Just one,' and as he calls, his flashgun floods the room with its light.

Later, in the picture he develops, the man imagines he can see the murdered woman's fingers, but even as he tries to convince himself of this he knows that what he is seeing is nothing more than a trick of the chemical light which has traced a dark edge to her outline and brought the faded flowers of the carpet into sharp relief.

10

The beauty contest had originally been intended as the centrepiece of the club's New Year's Eve celebrations, an oasis in its desert of winter, and had been open only to local women; afterwards, when the number of entrants declined, anyone prepared to pay the entrance fee and travel became eligible to participate. Last New Year's Eve there had been twenty-two entrants; this New Year's Eve there were sixteen. The council committee responsible for the event – and responsible, too, ultimately, for Mitchell and his failed club (which many of the committee members still referred to as the town's ballroom, blindly remembering its thirty-year-past heyday) – had tried to insist on the competition being open only to women living in the county. Mitchell had agreed. It was a large county. Then that bad decision had been annulled, and Mitchell had agreed to that too, swimming just beneath the surface and careful not to confront any of those splashing noisily above him.

Last year the winners of other competitions had entered; last year the winner of a regional television beauty show had entered. This year, not only had the woman refused an invitation to be one of the judges, but she had got married and pregnant and her life had skipped happily off in another direction completely.

'So who's going to win?' Laura called out.

Mitchell remained at the centre of the stage. 'How should I know?' The jury, in addition to Mitchell and the town mayor, was composed of various other local dignitaries and businessmen, mostly interchangeable these days, and the recently widowed wife of the man who had owned most of the town's amusement arcades, and who, before his death, had pushed hard for the new leisure centre. He normally participated himself in the show, returning each year from his hacienda dream-home in Spain, which he had owned for a decade, and where he had died. His widow – it was common knowledge – had returned to close her fist on his remaining business affairs in the town and to grieve briefly and publicly in the cold and the rain, where her tears and concerns seemed somehow more appropriate.

'You know as well as I do.' Laura walked out on to the stage to join him. The mayor's granddaughter was a late entry.

'You talk as though it matters,' Mitchell said to her.

'It does to all the others who've entered.'

They both watched a man drag a mound of stacked chairs across the dance floor and begin to arrange them around its edges. The mayor had said — fair play and honesty and all that — that he would withdraw from the judging when his granddaughter was being considered.

'What's she like?' Laura said.

'If it's any consolation, she's good-looking, got a good figure and knows what to say. She's seventeen, for Christ's sake.'

He had already imagined the headlines in the local papers. His bad decisions would become scandals, his inadequacies corruption, his failures made as obvious as bruises on a face. And everyone who lived in the town, all those people who had never once come into the club, would feel the loss as something personal. Public money had been invested and lost; everyone had the right to feel cheated.

The first year, Laura herself had entered the competition, largely at Mitchell's insistence, and more to show willing than with any serious intent, and she had come fourth. But that, too, had been the result of duplicity on the part of the judges. She had never entered again.

'They all know how it works,' Mitchell said.

She couldn't deny this.

'What are *we* doing?' she said.

'I thought the swords.' He waited for her to object.

They had performed the sword cabinet illusion the

previous year, and the one before that. There were few other parts to the act Mitchell had developed over the years that could be successfully performed in front of such a large audience and in a room that size with so much else going on. He would wear a dinner jacket. She would wear her tight-fitting silver costume and black, glittering tights. Everyone would cheer at her first appearance. She would parade around the cabinet striking poses and then she would be shut inside it while Mitchell went through his routine of pushing in the swords.

Tonight, before and after the act, and before the beauty contest, a troupe of exotic dancers would perform. This was a first for the club. They, too, would be revealingly dressed, and the instant before each of their routines finished and the flashing lights went out on them, they would pull off the tops of their costumes to briefly – very briefly, stroboscopically briefly – expose their breasts before being plunged into darkness and running from the stage. Mitchell had fought with the committee to include them. It was of no concern to him now whether they performed or not. The other members had allowed themselves to be persuaded. Only the mayor, they decided, ought to be seen to remain opposed to the troupe.

'And has everyone else agreed to go through the motions, do you think?' She objected to the sword cabinet, but said nothing.

'Stop worrying. Wait until you see her. One of the other entrants is thirty-two.'

Laura was thirty-four. 'Cheers,' she said.

'What?'

She shook her head. She heard the pipes around the room rattle slowly into life as they warmed. Her breath plumed in the cold air. She was about to ask Mitchell something else concerning the evening when he walked away from her to the far side of the stage and returned pushing the sword cabinet ahead of him. It came noisily on its stiff castors. It had been six months since they had last performed the illusion. The box was black, studded with silver moons and stars. Black and silver, like her costume. She would remember the smell of the inside of the box for as long as she lived.

'Leave it where it is,' she told him.

It would not be needed on stage, nor would there be room for it, until the dancers had completed their first routine.

'I need to test it,' Mitchell said. 'We don't want any accidents, do we?'

'Ha ha,' Laura said.

The plywood door, split into two, hung open. Mitchell fetched his retractable swords. Yet more lights flickered into life around the room. Fruit machines added their own small, frantic patterns.

'Ladies and gentlemen,' Laura suddenly called out. She pirouetted and gestured around the cabinet, stopped as abruptly as she had started, and then climbed down from the stage.

'Come back,' Mitchell called to her. 'I need you inside the thing.'

'Pretend.'

Mitchell watched her cross the room. When he had first met her she had been another of those women with their uncertain dream of something and somewhere and someone else still intact. She needn't have stayed with him; she could have thrown herself on to solid ground any time during the past year. He wanted to shout something reassuring to her, but could think of nothing to say. The cabinet rattled beside him. He knew why she disliked it so much. He still carried with him the photograph he had taken of her in her mermaid's costume on the day they met. Time had raged like a war since then. Five years.

He went to the front of the stage, and mimicking the voice of the chairman of the tourism committee, shouted, 'Some nights we are temporarily resurrected, and some nights, ladies and gentlemen of the jury, another sturdy nail of indifference and hostility is driven well and truly home.' He trailed off into his own voice. He knew that 'hostility' was the wrong word.

Halfway across the room, Laura stopped walking. 'You never really tried, did you?' she called back to Mitchell without turning. She tried to remember when she had finally stopped loving him, uncertain if the moment was months or seconds old, or if it had even yet passed.

'Perhaps they'll come to some arrangement and keep you on,' he called down to her.

'Perhaps.' She resumed walking into the outer darkness of the room.

On stage, Mitchell continued going through his routine with the swords. The illusion might be stretched to twenty minutes if he made the effort, if he really tried, if twenty minutes in front of those restless and un-appreciative audiences ever seemed like anything less than an eternity.

11

'Never spoke about it, that's why you have to imagine.'

'I've read just about everything the papers had to say about the case.'

'What do they tell you? Nothing.'

What Mitchell didn't say was that he'd seen beyond the sensational reporting to the transcripts of Morgan's interviews.

'Same with Arbuckle, Fatty this, Fatty that. To read the papers you'd think the Devil had bred with a giant pig and that Arbuckle had been the result. *Truth*, that's what's at stake here. And the strange thing is, the fat man himself was never devoted to it. Declared innocent a first time of all those charges and still they condemned him. Another trial and he's found even more innocent, slate wiped double clean, and still he's left nailed up there. Morgan saw all that. Only thing between the truth and a lie is the man being told it. Arbuckle's advice to me – don't look so surprised – was never to trust anyone wholly devoted to the truth. Truth to most of the Kings was a cheap plate spinning on a thin stick.'

Mitchell looked outside. Shadows crossed the bright sunlight, filtering it in moving shapes through the dirty glass and lace curtain into the room.

'Would you have known if Morgan had been lying?' he said.

'Me personally? Perhaps.'

'Did he lie to the police?'

'I don't know what he told them. And afterwards it hardly mattered to make the distinction between his lies and the truth.'

'Oh?'

'Why bother? By then everything he did was a lie. You'd be surprised how many of the other Kings were disappointed that he didn't stand trial.'

'The publicity?'

'Saying they wanted the trial to give him a fair hearing, and all the time making their own calculations about what they were really getting out of it.'

'Did no-one think to stop my mother from—'

'There were a lot of children, all moving from act to act as required, a season here, season there, wherever they were needed.'

'He seemed genuinely fond of her.'

'I don't doubt it. Just don't tell me he treated her like his own daughter. Where the Kings were concerned, that wouldn't be a great recommendation.'

'It always seemed to me as though he wanted to get her as well as himself away from the publicity.'

'Perhaps.'

'Away from everyone hounding him.'

'If you say so.'

It was clear to Mitchell that Quinn was resisting being drawn into revealing his own true feelings about Morgan and his mother.

'Houdini lost his mother and it changed his entire life, turned him into a different man completely,' Mitchell said.

'Gave Morgan his big break, you mean. I know all that stuff. That's why you're here, remember?'

Mitchell nodded.

Quinn looked back to the photograph of himself and Arbuckle. 'Wait until you hear the rest of it. You won't have heard this from any of the others. I was there with Morgan at Arbuckle's mother's funeral because Morgan – Morgan who was out there to make it big in the films – was filling in his time by filling in graves. We lived in a single room then, smaller than this one, shared everything with a dozen others, half of them waiting for their own big breaks, and the other half recovering from them. I only went along with Morgan for the ride. He didn't even know whose grave he was digging and filling until we saw all the preparations and saw everyone arrive.

Morgan and two others. I waited with them. It started to rain and there was nowhere to shelter. I remember seeing Morgan with the rain running down his face and dripping off his chin like it was manna from Heaven. He pointed them all out to me, all the big names, actors, film people, society. To hear him talk, you'd think they were going to wave him over to them, put their arms round his shoulders, wipe away his tears with their silk handkerchiefs and invite him to share in their grief like he was the only real friend any of them had ever had.'

12

From the moment he prised open the first of his mother's sealed chests and found the film of Clarence fired from his cannon, and imagined the watching girl that was his mother (already calculating her age and fitting her into the calendars of his search), Mitchell had understood that, more than anything else that had destroyed and scattered the Kings, their unstoppable decline had been fuelled first and foremost by their own cultivated, almost clinical, arrogance. And the further he searched, the more he convinced himself of this.

Right from the beginning, from the circuses, music halls and palaces of variety that had spawned and nurtured them, the Kings had been forever prodded with the double-edged and rubbery sword of shabby farce and tragedy; celebrating small gains and ignoring great losses; bowing at unexpected applause and ignoring the queues of disappointed people leaving the theatre early; collecting up the few bouquets that were thrown (as often as not by a planted King), but numb to their thorns, blind to the fact that the blooms were long past their prime, already more dead than alive; and deaf to the jeers and catcalls, and then later to the demands at the box office for money to be refunded.

Arrogance was the only word for it. After all, what did the Kings care, in the days of their ascendancy and triumphs, for the unfeeling world beyond the glare of the lights, beyond the expectant ripple of velvet curtains waiting only to be drawn aside for them to be revealed in all their glory?

Even then, half a century before Morgan, when the sword was first lifted and pointed in their direction, the Kings chose to ignore it; or, if they did not dismiss it completely, then they chose to look upon it as one more heartless prop, real and false, dangerous and harmless in equal measure, in that heartless world. Even then, in that life of endless celebrity bleeding into notoriety, they were rabbits circling ever closer to the centre of their field of harvested corn, avoiding all confrontation until the last possible moment, and all the while confident that when the time came for them to bolt they would make their escape and be once again admired and applauded for it.

But the bearers of the sword were many, and had become masters in its use. They may have used it indiscriminately in the beginning, wielding it as a child might swing a stick through a field of weeds, but later they became more determined, more selective, more expert in their prods and stabs and flourishes.

Later still, the sword was discarded and a guillotine wheeled centre stage. For a decade before Clarence and Morgan the Kings had been juggling with their own severed heads.

13 _____

Beyond the scene of the crime, beyond the red-lit room of the photographer, there is another room, windowless, unplastered brick thickly glossed in cream and green, a table, several chairs, papers, pens and photographs held flat beneath a palm on the table.

Morgan sits at one side of the table. He sits back from it, his legs stretched, his hands clasped, resting in his groin. Two men sit facing him, both junior to the man who took control in the room from which the body has already been removed. They sense a reluctance in Morgan, a feeling of ill-defined caution or alarm; and he, in turn, senses something of their eagerness, their anticipation.

This is the first time he and they have come together,

in silence, with intent, and all three of them are aware of the importance of beginning correctly, of observing the correct protocol.

A fourth man sits in the corner of the room, beyond the full glare of the central light in its wire cage, as blinding as any sun to look into directly. This man sits in a chair with a shelf attached, upon which rests his stenograph. Everything that is said in the room he translates in a succession of rapid and near-silent dabs and clicks as his fingers ripple left to right and right to left across his keys. Occasionally, one of the other three men glances across at him, watching to see that those fingers are still moving, but he is as quick as they are and they catch themselves in their own unmoving silences.

It is in his interrogation that past and future, fact and probability, supposition and hindsight all combine in Morgan's mind to create the fiction that everyone else was afterwards happy to accept.

The room still existed, and Mitchell had visited it. It had been empty then, disused, not even the table and chairs. The light no longer worked and its wire cage hung from the ceiling as though something had forced it open and escaped.

Morgan takes out a cigarette, and before lighting it, he turns it back and forth in a deft motion through his fingers, neither breaking nor even creasing it.

'A trick I picked up,' he says. He appears mesmerized by the simple, repetitive motion, reassured by it, as though it were something he had learnt as a child, something done with the deliberate intent of calming him, a rock around which to throw a rope and anchor himself.

He is watched closely by the two others. They know how much publicity the case has already attracted. They have come up the steps and through the waiting room filled with the clamour of the other Kings. They know he was with the woman on the evening prior to her death, that he was with her in the early hours. He has not denied this. Foundations are being laid. They know he gave her a photograph of himself, that he wrote on it. He has not denied this, either.

One of them tells him to stop playing with the cigarette and either light it or put it away. Morgan stops the instant he hears the note of rising anger in the man's voice, the cigarette between his fore- and index fingers, awaiting only to be raised to his lips, which he does.

The other man says, 'We can do without all the distractions.'

'Is it a distraction?'

'You know it is.'

'By which you imply what? That I am nervous – that I am frightened and hoping to disguise the fact? Or that I'm doing it merely to annoy you?'

'You tell us,' the man says. It is a disappointing, predictable reply, but in this way, throughout the days of his questioning, they move together and apart, small gains, small losses, connections made, connections guessed at, connections severed.

The photographs on the table have been fanned into a semicircle. Morgan has looked at them, but not too closely. A dozen pictures, all showing the same thing.

He is careful to tap all his ash into the tin ash-tray pushed across to him the instant he took out his cigarettes.

'Will you tell us again everything that passed between you and the young lady.'

'Oh, not again, surely.' The 'Oh' is another of his mannerisms. They have called him theatrical.

First thing that morning he had left London to travel to Southend on the train. As he had already explained, he had stayed on at his lodgings in London because the distance was so short and he would only be appearing in Southend – or not appearing, as now seemed to be the case – until the weekend. He had been met at the station, cautioned and escorted back to London.

Morgan leans forward, half-turning to rest his elbow on the table. You were there ahead of me, he tells them. You told me everything you knew, I told you everything I knew, and I agreed to come back with you on the train and to answer your questions so that a proper and official record might be kept of them. He is careful to look from one man to the other, to exclude neither. The way he might scatter his glances and smiles over a sparse but appreciative audience.

'I really do want to help you find that poor woman's . . .' He hesitates briefly before saying, 'killer', and then wonders if a less emotive word might not have been more suitable. His hesitation is noticed, and he considers if and how it will be understood and translated by the stenographer.

And as Morgan shifts his position at the table, so the two men alter theirs, remaining squarely in front of him as he turns.

'You must see it from our point of view,' one of them says. 'For all we know, you may already be responsible for the deaths of other young women. We already know that connections exist, and we know that the killer of one may be the killer of them all.'

I did no such thing. You are asking the wrong man. Morgan remains silent. His theatricality must be harnessed, must remain an asset. He will save it until he is vindicated.

'It was such a terrible return journey,' he says.

'Oh?'

'Short, but terrible. Absolutely.'

'Because you were being brought back here? Because you knew what lay ahead, not only an hour later back in London, but further ahead, years and years ahead?'

'No, of course not. Because of the suicide.'

There is a moment of uncertainty in the room, and uncertainty in that situation might easily turn to panic or failure.

No-one says, 'Suicide?' Instead, they let him go on.

The stenographer, taking advantage of the brief silence, lifts his fingers from the machine and flexes them to relieve them of some small occupational ache.

14

The first of the contestants arrived at six. Mitchell was back at the window overlooking the sea when the cars came. Laura sat behind him, close to a radiator. It had snowed earlier in the day and this now lay in lines and patches where it had not already been driven or trodden to slush. In places beneath the street lights it shone luminescent.

The summer illuminations had been switched back on for the night, and they alone created any sense of occasion. Birds and clowns and signs of the zodiac, some flashing in a semblance of movement, stretched left and right of the club along the Promenade. Mitchell regretted seeing the lights used like this. They were meant for warm summer evenings when the town was full of holidaymakers; now they only emphasized the sense of loss and waiting which coloured the winter.

One of the contestants looked up and saw Mitchell watching her. She recognized him and waved. Mitchell raised his hand in response.

'Who is it?' Laura said.

'No idea. They all look the same.'

'That's the point.'

'Will they come up here or go straight down to the dressing room?' he said.

'It's freezing down there.'

And as she spoke there was a knock at the door and one of the women came in, carrying a vanity case and a dress and a costume, both cellophane-wrapped. She hung these on the doorframe and went to Laura, complaining of the cold and of her long journey there.

She asked Mitchell if there had been many entrants.

'A fair few,' he said. Mostly non-runners, like yourself, he thought.

'Sixteen,' Laura said.

'I might have guessed.' The woman was nearer thirty than twenty. She had given her age as twenty-five. 'Still, it's all good experience.'

For what? Mitchell wanted to ask her.

'How do you rate my chances?' The woman bowed her head as she spoke, pretending to rub something from her leg, pretending that Mitchell and Laura did not share a glance over her head.

'Attractive personality like yours,' Mitchell said.

Laura pressed a finger to her lips.

'You said that last year.'

'Did I? And?'

'I wasn't placed.'

'I wasn't one of the judges then.'

The woman stood up and took off her coat. 'I've been working on my tan,' she said to Laura. She pulled up her skirt to reveal her legs and knickers.

'Nice,' Laura said.

'Salon. New technique. Fortune.'

Neither Mitchell nor Laura mentioned the mayor's granddaughter. The girl, still then at school, was shortly to leave and work as a demonstrator in the cosmetics department in a family-owned store in the town. She looked three years older than she was in the photograph she had unnecessarily submitted along with her application.

Below, others arrived. They congregated briefly in the cold and then came into the club. They too climbed the stairs to the flat. They greeted each other, quizzed each other, assessed their chances. When Mitchell suggested they go down to the dressing room, they complained that it was too early. Laura told them to stay where they were.

Mitchell poured himself a drink. He kept himself apart from them. He watched the explosion of foam beneath the swaying lights where the tide rolled up the curving wall and folded back on itself. The day, he sensed, had turned too quickly into night, without the easy hours of evening to mark its passing.

15

'When my father left I lived with my sister Mary. My mother was the King. Like you. And like you, my father couldn't stand the idea of it all. Every time she spoke of them he screwed up his face at the stink.'

'He left you?' Mitchell said.

'Prison. In and out. Said he was a burglar, but that was putting a spin on things. He once served two years for smashing a window and running off with nothing but a bleeding hand. Mary was seven years older than me. She lived not far from here. It was what brought me back here – not to this house – what would bring anyone here? – but to this part of London. Mary was married to Johnson. That was his Christian name, Johnson. She was the one who brought me up. Never been as close to anyone before or since.'

Except my mother, Mitchell thought.

'Johnson treated me like the son he could never have, and I had all the right bruises to prove it. He ruled over her, turned her into whatever he wanted her to be. You still see it happening, it's not that uncommon, even now. Melt a little, set hard in another shape.'

'You saw the same thing with my mother and father,' Mitchell said.

'Heard about it, guessed what was happening.' Quinn picked up a folded newspaper and fanned himself with it.

'Mary stuck it for five years and then walked out on him. It was the bravest thing she ever did.'

'And you went with her?'

'No. She went just like that. Waited for him to leave one morning, told me she would only be gone a minute, put on her coat and went.'

'But she got in touch with you afterwards?'

'No, not even that. She had to detach herself completely. Vanished. I never saw her again. The Kings never saw her again.'

'Did Johnson try and find her?'

'He made all the right noises. His was the loss, see. Everybody felt sorry for him. They had no idea how he treated her.'

'And you heard nothing at all?'

'She sent two postcards. One a year afterwards, the next three years after that. Still got them. Didn't say much, but I learned them off by heart. I couldn't believe she'd do that to me. She walked out on me and it was like an eclipse of the sun. I went looking for her, of course I did, but I was still only a child. Johnson sent the police after me, said I'd run away. I ended up in a home. And after that, another, then another. The authorities contacted my mother's relatives. Some of them came to visit me, Morgan among them. A couple offered to take care of me – I'm still not certain exactly who they were – cousins of Morgan's perhaps – and I went to live with them. The day after I arrived, Morgan came and took me from them. It had all been worked out between them. I was eleven. You have to remember that all this happened only a year after the First War. Everything was still up in the air. They lost orphans like me in their hundreds. I went to live with Morgan in a succession of places. He was travelling, then. You can imagine the appeal of that kind of life after what I'd been through. I once asked him if he knew anything of Mary. He said he didn't, but told me not to worry, and I always thought he knew something, that one day he'd somehow bring her back to me. He said we had to keep things quiet in case Johnson got to hear of what had happened.'

'And did he?'

'I doubt it. And if he did, he didn't care enough to do anything about it. I became Morgan's so-called assistant, just as your mother did later, and after a year moving around with him, we went to America in a bundle with twenty or thirty others.'

'Did you try looking for Mary when you came back?'

'I wanted to, but the first attempt I made, I inadvertently found my father. He was a drunk by then, trying to sponge off the Kings. It scared me to see him and I backed off. If I was going to hear anything about Mary that I didn't want to hear, then the last person I wanted to hear it from was him.'

'You thought she might be dead?'

'Or worse. Forgive the melodrama.'

'Did you imagine she was dead?'

'It's what I let myself think and then go on believing.'

'She'll be dead by now, surely?'

'Why don't you just punch me in the face?' Quinn said.

Mitchell apologized.

'Of course she's dead. You've only got to look at me. I'm dead and she's deader. I used to convince myself that by coming back here after America I might one day see her and that everything would be all right again, that we'd have some sort of life together.'

'And it never happened.'

'Like lots of things never happened. Like they never happened for me, never happened for Morgan, never happened for any of them.'

The photograph of Quinn with Roscoe Arbuckle was in Mitchell's hand. He studied it again in the light of all he had just learned. 'How soon after this did you come home?'

'Not long. We were back before everything blew up in that poor fat bastard's face. I read all about it, couldn't miss it. I had my connection to it all, you might say. I showed it all to Morgan, but he wasn't interested. We neither of us knew it then, but we had thirty bad years ahead of us. We survived, but that's about all.' He took the picture from Mitchell and looked at it. 'He cried like they were burying everyone he had ever known. Morgan lifted me up on to a life-size marble angel and I could see his big glossy bladder of a face trembling and wet with the tears. I could even see where they soaked into his shirt. You'd think it might be rain, but all the studio men around him kept umbrellas over the umbrellas over his head. He cried then, but he never cried afterwards. Not even when they crucified him, not even then, not a single tear.'

Quinn started to shake gently where he sat.

A message was passing along the lines and it shook them with the flight of its invisible news.

16

It was of paramount importance to Houdini that the cabinet in which he might or might not perform his illusion should be standing upright, and that he should remain visible within its glass walls throughout the time the ice formed around him. His designs and calculations revealed in every detail how the illusion was to be accomplished.

Reading these, it was easy for Mitchell to understand how Morgan must have felt upon seeing them for the first time, and as the notion to duplicate the illusion took place in his own mind.

An inner and outer mould were to be constructed, both of sheet glass of varying thickness and strength, with both moulds held in place by wooden clamps and pins.

There were to be no screws in the contraption, only these slotted pins, whose weakness under pressure from the expanding ice would act as a safeguard, something which might then afterwards be exploited.

The space inside the inner, thicker mould was to be the smallest possible, and the case was to be built to the dimensions of Houdini's chained body. (As ever, the chains would be of no consequence; when the time came they would slide to his feet. There were to be ropes, too, under the chains, but these were intended to remain attached to his wrists and ankles, adding to the spectacle of him smashing his way alive out of the ice.)

Air would be fed into the inner mould through a hose attached to a mouthpiece. No secret would be made of this while the ice was forming. It would afterwards be removed and displayed alongside the cabinet while Houdini remained inside, his salvation so close and yet so far. What *was* to be kept secret was the second hose, built into the frame of the structure, which would feed warm air into the inner mould from beneath.

The gap between the two glass cases was then to be filled with crushed ice which would settle and compact. Cold air would be blown on to the outer mould to help this process. The glass walls would cause the ice to form into a block. At no point was the distance between the inner and outer cases more than six inches.

As it formed and thickened, the ice would grow opaque, and this would add further to the illusion; except directly in front of Houdini's face, where the mould was thin, and where, using two hidden glass barriers, cold water would be allowed to settle so that Houdini's eyes might be visible throughout. A pickaxe was to be 'frozen' into the inner mould with him. Again no secret would be made of this, though how a man whose limbs were supposedly held by the forming ice would be able to help himself was another matter. For Houdini, the key to the illusion rested on the secrecy of the inner chamber, and on the rate of freezing and the 'localization' of the ice in the space between the moulds.

As little warm air as possible was to be used – only that amount required to maintain a reduced body temperature was to be fed in, and then only when instructed by Houdini via his mouthpiece.

For a year beforehand he prepared himself for the illusion by immersing himself in baths of ice, timing and pushing forward the limits of his endurance. His glaziers built a bath within a bath, whereby hardly any of the crushed ice and freezing water came into direct contact with his skin.

To assist in the eventual break-up of the ice, concealed metal rods would also be built into the wooden frame of the structure. These would further act as blades to help shatter the ice, and their pressure would create significant weaknesses in the forming 'block', which, even upon completion, would remain considerably less solid and massive than the audience had been led to believe. These metal rods were designed to fall into the base of the structure when Houdini emerged, and stay hidden there amid the pieces of shattered ice.

The crushed ice was to be poured into the mould at several points, ensuring, as far as this was calculable or possible, an even distribution of compaction and build-up. It would be impossible to complete the illusion were the ice to form only from his feet upwards, and to this end, other concealed glass plates were fitted between the two cabinets to allow a more controlled consolidation. Like the metal rods, these plates were designed to fall into the base of the frame and be lost there.

There was some possibility, there being so much glass used in the construction of the cabinet, that Houdini might suffer from being cut. With other illusions he had prepared his skin to minimize the extent of any bleeding, but on this occasion the full effect of the shattering ice and glass – which needed to be as spectacular as possible – remained incalculable. A month was spent experimenting with water frozen on to glass which was then smashed. Houdini was confident that the bulk of the shattered glass would fall away from him, and that the ice adhering to the outer wall of the inner chamber would offer him further protection.

As much trapped air as possible was to be incorporated into the growing block. To achieve this, Houdini would employ five or six assistants filling the mould continuously and quickly until it overflowed. A simple scaffold would be wheeled into place on either side of the cabinet to allow these assistants access, and then be wheeled away when their work was finished.

The fans blowing cold air into and on to the mould would be in operation long before the illusion was introduced. Houdini had four of these fans built for him by a company specializing in meat refrigeration. He also discussed with them the possibility of using an electrically driven refrigeration unit to assist with the freezing. Several additional blueprints were drawn up, but the major problem with these was that it would have been difficult to keep the effects of the freezing away from Houdini's body. Several experiments which quickly converted sides of beef to stone convinced him not to pursue the idea. Besides which, an ice machine – in the eyes of a sceptical public – might also provide him with air and warmth, might generate the power to eventually shatter the ice and free him. He wanted none of this. The strength and appeal of the illusion remained in the simplicity – he wanted people to believe in its crudity – of the attempt. He wanted people to be able to imagine themselves coming up with a similar scheme, and any specialized machinery would destroy all that.

Once in position, and with the crushed ice and freezing water already being poured, Houdini would slide a glass shelf over his head. Invisible drainage holes were drilled into the base of the inner structure to ensure that any water seeping in could also drain away. Some among his team remained sceptical regarding these drains once the ice at the bottom of the mould had started to form.

Houdini was exhorted to wear a pair of knee-length insulated and watertight boots but this too he knew would detract from the seeming simplicity and danger of the illusion. He would wear only his trademark belted trunks.

The real test, once the shelf over his head was in position, was then a simple one of endurance. If the ice formed too quickly or expanded by a greater degree than was calculated, then the outer, thinner mould might shatter too early. On the other hand, if the ice took too long to form, other, hitherto unidentified, weaknesses might be revealed, followed by damage to the inner mould. Everything was designed from strength to weakness in an attempt to channel and constrain the forming ice.

It remained vital for that ice to at least appear to have formed into a solid block – solid enough for him to seem to be firmly encased within it, and afterwards solid enough to shatter when the time came for him to release himself. Too much water, and the inner casing and metal rods would be revealed. Too much ice, too densely and too quickly formed, and Houdini would be unable to shatter it from within and step out.

His release remained the final part of the challenge. The assistants, having finished pouring the water and crushed ice, and having removed the scaffold, would then return to the stage to stand on either side of him with sledgehammers at the ready. Their staring, unmoving presence would contrast markedly with what appeared to be the struggle of the man within the ice.

The illusion, however, would be better accomplished if the hammers were not used, and to this end a method of emergency self-release was devised. This consisted of two hinged metal rods concealed in the lower half of the inner casing. By drawing up on these Houdini could force them out through the inner mould, allow them to connect with the rods already concealed there, and then use this pressure, along with the weight of the formed ice, to shatter the thinner, weaker, outer glass. If, in the event, this was not wholly successful, having created himself a little more room for manoeuvre, Houdini could also use the ice axe to further effect his escape.

Were the outer mould to creak or even to crack during the illusion, then this would only add to the drama, allowing the audience to imagine that same pressure being simultaneously exerted on the body of the man inside.

In Morgan's attempt almost thirty years later, it had been Mitchell's mother's role to act as a distraction to the men filling the mould, dancing around the cabinet in her silver feathers and cape, while inside Morgan counted off the minutes to his release. In addition, there was to be some suggestion to the watching audience that this small dancing girl, charm and grace circling the monolith, was also the daughter of the man they might have believed to be already beyond their prayers.

17 _____

KILLER SOUGHT. FIND THIS MAN. BRUTAL SLAYING.

One headline as good as any six others, all interchangeable, all prolonging the inevitable.

'Bloody good picture, bloody good composition, front page, definitely, no question, bloody good the way that shoe was left to hang. You can't see her head, but you can make out the shape of it.'

The shadowed peak of her nose, the shallow crater of her open mouth where the sheet has been drawn in slightly, as though she had breathed her last only after it had been pulled over her.

'You'd think they'd have more bloody sense and get everything covered up right from the start. We got her full name? Age? They want telling about that.' The editor is a happy man. Murders sell newspapers, and his newspaper was the best at selling murders, the facts of the matter kept as simple as possible, fleshed out with outrage and the unimaginable made visible.

'I tried to get some more, but they weren't having any of it,' the photographer says. 'I offered to do some for them, but their own man was there before me. Said they had all they needed. I know him, he won't sell.'

'They'll want them to rub in the face of some poor bloody jury.'

They would want them long before that.

The photographer has shown no-one the picture of the woman's imaginary fingers against the threadbare bouquets. He has kept that one for himself. His own imagination has been at work, his own dreams invaded. Her feet have moved, her fingers have beckoned him, and the living and the dead have already begun their careful dreaming dance. The editor slaps him on the back. The room around them is marbled with smoke and people cross it in all directions holding up sheets of paper and shouting at each other.

'We're on the case. It's all yours. There's already a whisper that the bloke might have killed before. And if he has . . .'

They wanted to know about it. Their readers wanted to know about it. It was their right to know and the newspaper's duty and responsibility to tell them.

'Bastard.'

After this, the pace begins to quicken.

The photographer spends two sleepless nights with the photograph of the woman's feet on the floor beside his bed. His rented room is not dissimilar to her own.

Once, on the uncertain boundary between sleeping and waking, he calls out for her to stop. He examines the stains on his own sheets and the sweat which now gathers in his palms on even the coldest of nights.

18

If the older Kings could never deny their blood, then some of the younger ones, the ones Mitchell eventually came to meet, the ones moving to the edges of the out-of-control merry-go-round and steadying themselves to jump off, were never so convinced. They knew that the world no longer needed acrobats, jugglers, escapologists, knife-throwers and illusionists, that what it needed then were accountants and consultants, systems experts and analysts, men who could destroy that old order and build anew.

For the older generations of Kings, all that mattered was for there to be a crowd demanding to be entertained, to be made to laugh or scream, or to cry out with disbelief or to have the breath jolted from their bodies.

Mitchell knew long before his own indirect involvement with them that they were a doomed race, that the roots of their tree were already dead, and that the rot was being drawn up into the trunk even as the higher, greener branches struggled upwards to the cooling sun. He accepted then that there was to be no real escape for any of them – himself and his dead mother included – and that when the body corporate finally succumbed they would all be brought down and be destroyed or maimed by it.

In the beginning, he was alarmed and confused by this uncertain understanding, but gradually it offered a shape and a course to his life and thoughts.

He knew he was not the first of them to have worked this out, and that others had run further than he had run, but in all his enquiries he had come across no-one who had admitted to this, no-one who had refused outright to tell him what they knew or remembered of Morgan, their father's cousin once-removed, their mother's sister's brother-in-law, friend of a relative, blood on blood, relative of a friend.

It did not matter to him that the ropes frayed and unravelled at the touch of his questions, only that he saw them do this, and that he occasionally felt the tatters and the dust fall through his own fingers instead of through the failing memory of someone else.

19

'Tell me, is this honestly what you expected to find, all this?' Quinn gestured at the room around him.

'I was just pleased to have found *you*,' Mitchell said.

'Found me alive, you mean.'

Mitchell conceded this in silence.

'And if not me, then anyone else who could tell you what you wanted to know.'

'I don't know who else there is.' Of the sixty letters he had written asking for assistance and information, Mitchell had received only eleven replies, and five of those from the quintuplet sisters of the same family, each one of them repeating what the others had already said. It was upon visiting the women, and the few other respondents, that Mitchell had become even more convinced of the need to discover if Quinn were still alive and then to find him. With Quinn he had a hold on both Morgan and his mother.

'You only have to look around you,' Quinn said.

'I didn't know what I'd find.'

'There are homes.'

'Homes?'

'For the Distressed Gentlefolk of the Theatrical and Entertainment World. Something like that.'

'Did you consider it?'

'I doubt I'd be eligible. Besides, it would be like living in a museum.'

'Did you resent or regret not having made it bigger in America?'

'Bigger? I didn't even make it small. Ad work, voices, that's barely even making it at all.'

'Some of the Kings must have made money somewhere.'

'They did. The circus Kings.'

'Did they own a circus?'

'No. We called them that because they were the performers who signed regular contracts for circus work, travelling around, dependable for seven or eight months each year. The rest of the Kings looked down on them. Morgan certainly did. He said they were no better than the animals in the cages. *We* were independent artistes dictating our own terms. Struggling and starving on our own terms, more like.'

'Was the circus money good?'

'Average. But it was there. And the more astute ones bought into the operations. They were big earners in the Fifties and Sixties, circuses. Even now, with the right management a circus is a profitable operation. They made even more money when they sold off their winter quarters to the developers. Your mother had a cousin, Courageous Charles King, started out as an acrobat and broke both his legs and both his arms in a bad fall. He'd put a bit aside, no wife, no kids, and when he mended he bought a wintering ground on the Isle of Dogs and ran it as the off-season manager' – Mitchell looked up at this – 'for a big-name circus. First thing he did was cut it in half and sell half to a business consortium. That was his first fortune. Five years later, the council tell him they're going to buy the other half off him – compulsory purchase. Docklands. He refuses, holds out, good lawyer, and two years after that they pay him ten times what they first offered. *And* they find him a new ground, rent-free, for the caravans and animals.'

'I saw the five Nightingale Sisters,' Mitchell said.

'Regulars at the Hoxton Britannia.'

'Their father was Oscar King.'

'I knew Oscar well. In fact, he once worked the cannon which later fired poor Clarence into the mud.'

'Is he still alive?'

'You're probably talking about Oscar Junior, his son. First boy to each member of the family was named Oscar.'

'It might be the same man.'

'The daughters all still alive?'

'A year ago they were.'

'Then it's his father I'm talking about.'

Mitchell began to sense that they were wandering too far along another of those divergent paths. 'What happened after the cigar commercial?' he said.

'Work for a few more months. Set-building and grave-digging. A day or two here and there as extras. We must have appeared in twenty films between us.'

'You and Morgan?'

'Together in some of them.'

'You actually appeared—'

'Just that. Face in the crowd. Passer-by. Man with newspaper. Come and gone. Never any credit. We worked through an agency. But as far as Morgan was concerned it was still a big step in the right direction. He used to sit up all night sending out letters and photographs to the casting people. That was when he wanted me to make something of the Arbuckle picture.'

'It might have been worth a try.'

'I didn't want anything to do with it. Remember the Mexican?'

'The woman?'

'I had something with her. Not much, but I got it because of what I was. Mister Cigar himself, he'd had his fill of her, so to speak. It turns out she wasn't from Mexico at all, but from Hungary. Can you credit that? Her father was a chicken farmer.' Quinn spoke now as though he were remembering these things for the first time in seventy years. 'It didn't last. It's hard to say what happened to her after the cigar ad. I never saw her on the screen again. You can imagine. One winner, a thousand losers.'

20

The club doors were opened at seven. The entertainment began an hour later. A local comedian and a local band entertained the growing crowd. It surprised Mitchell to see how many people had turned out. Pound of flesh, he supposed. The local newspaper had been dropping hints about his alleged mismanagement for over a month.

The mayor and his family, among the first to arrive, sat around four tables at the front of the room. The other judges took up their own reserved positions. The mayor attracted Mitchell's attention as he came close to them and beckoned him over. A man rose beside the mayor, and Mitchell saw the camera round his neck and recognized him as a reporter and photographer for the town's paper. The mayor shook Mitchell's hand and the man took pictures of the two of them together. The mayor repeated loudly that in the interests of fair play he would not be casting a vote for his granddaughter when the time came. There could be no misunderstanding. The photographer took out a notebook and wrote in it. The mayor spelled out his granddaughter's name, holding on firmly to Mitchell's hand as he spoke. Interests of fair play, he said again. There was the man's headline.

Even these dead rivers of history, Mitchell realized, must have their tired witnesses.

'And will we be graced by the presence of the beautiful Laura?' the mayor said, releasing his grip on Mitchell.

'Been looking forward to seeing you all day,' Mitchell said. He scanned the room round them as he spoke, but saw no sign of her.

'The pleasure's all mine,' the mayor said. 'Tell her to come over. You know where we are.'

'Oh, I always know that,' Mitchell said. His smile came to him as naturally as a growl to a dog.

The smile on the mayor's face wavered. He motioned the reporter away from them. 'And it's something you'd do well never to forget. You and I are going to be seeing a lot of each other after tonight.' As he spoke, the mayor waved and nodded to people passing by them.

Music suddenly sounded from the speakers at the front of the stage, making further conversation difficult.

'I have to go,' Mitchell said, deliberately lowering his voice.

'What?'

Mitchell left him and went in search of Laura.

He found her upstairs. She was alone now, all the contestants having gone down to the dressing room. She stood where he had stood earlier, at the window, staring out at the blackness as though something impossibly distant might be revealed to her there. The circling beam of the lighthouse burst against the glass and cast her in silhouette as she turned to him. She drained the glass she held.

'The dancers are on soon,' he said to her.

Laura poured herself another drink. Mitchell tried not to watch her. He knew how she felt about the sword cabinet.

'Are you okay? For the act?'

'Am I sober, you mean.'

'I won't drag it out,' he said. 'Ten minutes.'

'How sober would I have to be to stand upright in a box and keep my mouth shut?'

'Fifteen at the most.'

'Take as long as you like. After all, it will be our very own little Grand Finale.'

'Not necessarily,' he said, but could not bring himself to look at her as he spoke.

She had already made up her face and put on her wig. She left the window and came closer to him.

'Save it for them,' she said. 'Don't lie to me.'

She wore a dressing gown with a padded heart stitched over its breast pocket. She'd made a joke of this when she'd bought it. A year ago, during an argument, she'd torn the heart off and thrown it at him. She remembered him flinching as it hit him and then looking down to where it lay at his feet.

The next time he had seen her in the dressing gown the heart was back in place.

Her costume for that evening lay across an ironing board. She smoothed the creases from her shining tights.

Mitchell poured himself a drink and offered the bottle back to her. She took it but stood it beside her without pouring from it.

'What's going to happen?' she said eventually. 'I mean really happen.'

'I don't know.'

'Yes you do.'

'I don't—'

'You've made plans.'

'Plans for what?'

'For what happens next.'

'I don't know what you're talking about.'

Another sword fight of a conversation.

'Is it a lot of money?'

'I'm not certain. Yes. It isn't there for me to count it.'

'But enough for them to want to try and get it back from you. Enough for them to come after you.'

'Come after me?'

'The police.'

'It would have happened already.'

'You think they'll want to keep it quiet?'

'What did they honestly expect of a place like this?' he said.

'As much as you expected from it when you took it on, presumably.'

The divided percentages of all costs and profits had been calculated to two decimal points from the very beginning.

The police had been to see him, but only informally. No charges had yet been laid. Those, if they came, would have to await the full investigation and audit which was coming in three days' time, when the limbo of the holiday finally ended.

'How clean are the books?' Laura said.

'More tidy than clean.'

'But not tidy enough to fool anybody who knows what they're looking at for very long?'

'Ten, fifteen seconds.'

'It's not much of a start.'

They both smiled at this. Even through the growing space of their drift apart there were still these moments of affection.

'What will it be, fraud, embezzlement, theft?'

'They might want to try a bit of each.'

'So where will you go?'

'Go?'

'Don't. Where? Back to London?'

Mitchell made a clicking sound.

'It's where you always go. You might make a big point of denying it, but everything you know is there.'

Another click.

'You should never have left there in the first place. And wherever you went, the last place you should ever have come was here.'

He would never admit it, but he was grateful to her for what she forced him to face.

'You're worried in case I start asking you to let me come with you,' she said.

'We can forget the act,' he said.

'Which one? This one, or the swords?'

'I'm sure they'd all be more than happy to go straight from the dancers to the swimwear.'

The noise of the concert hall below rose up to them – occasional words, the voice of the comedian, outbursts of laughter and short silences.

'I want to do it,' she said.

'There's every chance they'll keep you on,' he said. 'You'll be an asset. You know how the dump runs.'

'No they won't. All I know is how everything fell apart. They'll want a clean start.'

'You could tell them what they'd never find in a year of looking.'

She shook her head. She took out a piece of paper from her heart pocket. 'Did you know that twelve of the entrants have put down their profession as beautician.'

'And whose interests include feeding the hungry, housing the homeless and praying for world peace. What did the mayor's granddaughter put?'

'Student.'

They both laughed.

Mitchell put his arm around her. 'There's nothing I can do,' he said.

She had not believed such a blackness could exist, the blackness outside, the blackness of the sword cabinet, the blackness of the future, and the blackness of her own torn heart. She turned into him and slid her arms around him. 'I know,' she said.

21

Why does he have to behave like that?

Behave like what?

Those gestures, mannerisms. None of it helps.

Helps what?

Helps them.

Helps them what?

That. That. Behave like that.

Because it is the way I am, Morgan said. The way I am.

Twelve hours have passed and they are tiring of him. He continues to insist on his innocence. The two junior detectives have grown braver in their questioning, but so far all they have accomplished is to re-establish ten times over everything they already knew. One of the men slaps the table with his palm.

Histrionics, Morgan thinks.

'You, my friend, are in serious trouble.'

Oh, so he's their friend now, is he?

'I've told you everything I know. I met her, we spoke, she dropped her scarf, I tried to find her, couldn't.'

'But then, according to your first story, you intended taking the scarf back to the club cloakroom.'

'That was a lie.'

'We know it was a lie.'

'I always meant to keep it.'

'We know that, too. What we want to know now is, why?'

The predictability of the pattern continues to reassure him.

'I just kept it,' he said. 'She was a very attractive young woman.'

'We know she was. Attractive in what way?'

'Attractive attractive.'

'Over-half-your-age attractive?'

'That had no bearing.'

'We think it did.'

'Then you're wrong.'

'If you insist.'

He asked them for another cigarette, an endless supply.

'We're finding out about you,' the man said as he held out his lighter.

'What are you finding out?'

'You get around a lot.'

'It's the nature of my profession.'

'To places where other, similar crimes have been committed.' To where they may be committed in the future.

'I dare say the same might be said of millions.'

'You're wrong there. Most people follow very exact routines, day in, day out, barely a foot either side of the path.'

Like you, Morgan thought.

'You lived in America for several years. Why was that?'

'I was engaged in the motion-picture industry there. In its infancy then, of course.'

'What films were you in?'

'It was thirty years ago.'

'We know when it was.'

'I was disappointed in my—'

'I bet you were.'

'And so I—'

'And so you came back here and took up where you left off.'

'I wouldn't put it quite like that.'

'Then how would—'

'I dug graves.' And for an instant he is lost.

'You what?'

'Excuse me.'

'You said you dug graves.'

'Briefly. Yes. For a living. A few months – weeks, no more.'

'You were a gravedigger?'

'It was never how I saw myself.'

But they had found something in the moment of his

reverie, of his footsteps in that distant country, and they did not want to lose their advantage. Soon their superior officer would be coming to join them. They wanted to have something to give him, to prove their worth. They wanted him to be proud of them, like a father proud of his sons.

'I dug holes in the ground. You might say I was a labourer.'

'It's a skilled job, grave-digging. Anybody who wanted, say, to bury a body, it wouldn't be an easy thing to do.'

'Why not?'

'It just wouldn't.'

He was a gravedigger, they'd say, ignoring the chasm of years. He was a gravedigger. They did not want to remember, to have to consider how poorly some of the bodies had been hidden from sight.

'So why would a theatrical dig graves?'

'I've explained.'

'You needed the money. Still, good experience.'

They batted every one of his deflections straight back at him.

One of the two men studied a sheaf of papers. He laid these down on top of the photographs.

'You told the arresting officer—'

'The man who met us from the train.'

'You told him you were an escapologist.'

'That's correct.'

'Were you telling the truth?'

'Of course.'

'You know we're searching your lodgings.'

'You said.'

'And you have no worries, no fears concerning what we might find there?'

'None at all.'

'So, what did you do as an escapologist?' the man asked him.

Morgan began to explain, bracing himself against what he knew must come next. What he told them sounded unreal to them.

These are the facts as gathered: Eileen Louise Beresford, aged twenty-one.

'I was telling you earlier about the train,' Morgan said.

'No you weren't. You were telling us about what you did.'

'But the train was important.'

'No it wasn't.'

'Like Houdini,' the second man said suddenly, the name hitting Morgan like a blow in the chest.

'Yes, like Houdini,' he said. Less than a fortnight had passed since his last visit to Cecil Court. Better than Houdini.

The two junior detectives shared a glance and a smile.

'It makes a change from an out-of-work docker beating his common-law wife to death because she went on at him about his drinking.'

'What?'

'Did you tell *her* what you did?'

'Who?'

Eileen Louise Beresford, aged twenty-one.

'We talked mostly about her. She was having some problems.'

'Aren't we all? Still, they're over now.'

Houdini.

'What are?'

'Her problems. I said they're over now.'

'I suppose so.'

The light above them flickered briefly and then regained its brilliance.

'It happens all the time,' the second junior detective said, and he looked to the silent stenographer to ensure that the man was keeping up with them.

22

His mother left him four sealed tea chests, each packed as tight as an egg. The accompanying letter, given to him at the reading of her will, indicated that the chests were for him alone, that no-one else was aware of their existence, and that no-one else, including Mitchell's father, had ever even seen them.

His father was reputed to have been a medal-winning swimmer, a school and county champion, but he had refused to speak about it to Mitchell as a boy, and had done nothing to encourage his own interest in the sport. Everything Mitchell had learned, he had learned from his mother, and he was sworn to secrecy by her as she taught him, as though every detail shared with him was one more skin removed from a terrible secret.

He remembered how inexplicably proud he had been of her, seeing her in her own costume when they went swimming together, how perfectly formed and trim she seemed to him beside the mothers of the other boys. Her costumes, too, had always been better fitting, more fashionable, more daringly coloured or patterned. But he had not then understood why this was, why such details still mattered to her; nor had he the slightest idea, he afterwards realized, of what thoughts and memories were passing through her own mind as she sat at the edge of the pool, her cap tight against her head, calling to him, her only child, her feet kicking in the water and then raised and folded neatly beneath her chin to make her a girl again.

Who, now, apart from the historians and the collectors of that paraphernalia, even remembers the Kings?

Morgan's death was reported on the front page of four national newspapers – 17 May 1954 – and on the inside pages of at least a dozen others. It was news in the trade papers for weeks afterwards.

The name might stir some vague memory amid all the lesser royalty of Prince This and Queen That, and some dim shape – Morgan himself, perhaps – might rise up to the echo of a handclap before sinking slowly back into the shadows again.

The Kings – and Mitchell had understood this from the start, too – were exotic birds in a drab world, as worn but as appropriate as the threadbare comparison, ready to die of neglect, or, failing that, of delusion, stunning for the moment they spread their wings and shimmered and flew, but then all too easily caught and crushed by their own preening vanity.

It was reported that over two hundred wreaths were laid at Morgan's grave, and that from a distance the ground into which his coffin was lowered two months after his death resembled a spectacular municipal garden in its ostentation and colour, a fire of the yellows, reds and blues so beloved of the Kings, and so vital a part of them before they wandered out into the glare of condemnation and started to fade.

23 _____

'What is there left worth having or holding on to?' he had said to her six months earlier when the full extent of his mismanagement had first become public knowledge, when it had been revealed and dragged out into the light of indignation and outrage and then shaped into a target for retribution. 'You won't get any choice,' Laura told him then. 'Jump or get pushed. Either way, it's still only *you* doing the plummeting-helplessly-to-earth bit.'

She waited for him to perhaps say, 'And you', and would deliberately misunderstand him and tell him of her own non-existent plans for the future. He had been saved then by the onset of the summer and the need to make what he could of it. Everything – or everything he knew might be discovered — was known, but he had not yet been confronted directly with the evidence. He had told her then to act as though nothing was wrong. She'd been doing that ever since she met him, she said. Ever since the sharks.

Even then, six months ago, he had been calculating his routes of denial. Laura's best advice to him had been to start throwing dirt. There were things he knew, things they both knew, about the members of the council and their dealings elsewhere in the town. He had agreed with her, briefly deceiving her into believing that their withdrawal was based on a joint strategy, that they were both involved. In a place like that, she said, and with people like them, a lot of anything thrown was going to stick. But Mitchell knew that it was what they expected him to do. Fires were already being lit in metal waste bins after office hours, men were talking to each other through car windows, games of golf were being played, promises and lies becoming interchangeable.

They'd be ready for anything, he told her. Too predictable. But you're a predictable man, she had said. Always have been. That's why all this has happened.

And so predictability became his stratagem.

It was after speaking to her, both of them awake through a short summer night, that, in the silence of his preparations, he had decided to leave her behind.

For her part, Laura understood this. Something else unspoken. Not wanted on journey. Dead weight.

And for those six months the cruelties, manoeuvrings and deceptions had grown like beautiful crystals, intricate and ever-extending, and ready to shatter at the first sharp tap of unguarded truth.

24

'That other fat one, Oliver Hardy, see how he ended up. What a waste, what a tragedy. Who sees these things coming? Not me, that's for sure. And certainly not you.'

'Me?' The remark caught Mitchell unawares.

'Yes, you. Don't pretend you knew you were going to find out even the smallest part of any of this when you first started looking.'

'I had a good idea from everything I knew about my mother, everything she left me.'

'You got the pieces, that's all. Are you married?'

'I was.'

'And now?'

Mitchell thought of Laura. 'Nobody.'

'And for a living?'

He told Quinn about the club.

'I did a summer season there once. There's a pier.'

'Demolished about ten years ago.'

'An end-of-pier show. Good work.'

'With Morgan?'

'No, another escapologist, "Goodbye George". George King. Your mother will have known him. I trussed him up, put him in his sacks, boxes, whatever, and while he was getting himself free I got the audience to yell out "Goodbye, George" to him. Never loud enough so I ask them to shout again. By which time he's out of everything, down the trapdoor and standing behind them. I doubled up with a few other acts.'

'My mother's first appearance with Morgan after his release was on Cromer Pier,' Mitchell said.

'I know. I was there.'

'Working?'

'In the audience. I wanted to see what he had her doing.'

'Which was?'

'She was what, thirteen, fourteen, so it must have been during the school holidays. She didn't do much, just danced around him, helped him in and out of things. He was out of condition. Even then he was having trouble with his joints and his breathing. Occupational hazard, I suppose. The one thing an escapologist can live without – especially one who thought as much of himself as Morgan did – is stiff joints. It's why he went in for more and more elaborate stunts, why he stopped fighting his way out of strait-jackets and chains and started looking around for something more impressive.'

'Did you make your true feelings about him known to the police when they interviewed you?'

'Not really. The Kings, remember? – all for one and one for all, especially if the one was Morgan. He was already billing himself as their salvation.'

'What did they ask you?'

'Just what I knew about him, where he'd been, if I'd been with him, here and in America.'

'Did they think you were still working together?'

Quinn paused before answering. He fumbled for his words. 'I – he – what I mean—' He looked at Mitchell as though wanting him to intervene. Mitchell said nothing. Quinn took several deep breaths before continuing. 'He told them we were sharing lodgings.'

'And you weren't?'

'Yes and no. He was working in Southend; he'd stayed with me for three or four nights before he was arrested. He had some of his clothes here, most of his stage stuff. He said he was between lodgings and work and needed somewhere to keep everything safe and to hand. A few days here, a few days there. It wasn't always easy to move in and out of lodgings at such short notice. He had other digs in Clacton, where he'd been working beforehand.'

'But he told the police he was living with you, not there.'

'The first I knew of it was when they knocked and said they had a search warrant.'

'So they searched only those of his belongings that were with you. And presumably they found nothing worth finding.'

'There was nothing *to* find.'

'And in his lodgings in Clacton?'

'They never went.'

'And you kept quiet. Didn't anyone else come forward who recognized him? His picture was in plenty of the papers at the time.'

'It looked nothing like him. He had a dozen names. And who else was there? How many times do you need telling that it was a different world?'

'You must have thought or known he had *something* to hide by him sending the police to you.'

'Why?'

'Then why not tell them about Clacton?'

'He told me afterwards he was doing it for your mother's sake. How much of an excuse do you think they'd need to take her away from him? She was in Clacton being looked after by one of his women friends. Rooms in a house. It wasn't difficult to hide someone, to keep your head down, but not with all that sort of attention. Everyone would have been round, police, newspapers, welfare societies, orphanage people. He said he was doing it for her, and I believed him.'

It was beyond Mitchell to press the point and expose the shading of these half-truths and fossilized convictions.

'I can appreciate your situation,' he said. The words sounded mocking.

'I doubt it,' Quinn said, and motioned as though to suggest he wanted to say no more on the subject. 'They still think Arbuckle did those things. You ask anybody today and that'll be all they remember of him. Everybody still thinks he was guilty and found guilty. The louder you shout, the more chance you've got of being believed. It was true then and it's true today. Sometimes the truth matters, sometimes it doesn't. Sometimes you get to decide what the truth is, sometimes it's someone else's turn to decide. Nobody's whiter than white, not you, not me, not him, not Morgan, but at least Arbuckle got a court – got *two* courts – to stand up and tell the world he was innocent – and look what still happened to him.'

And you remembered all this when they came for Morgan, Mitchell thought, but said nothing.

'I telephoned your mother while they were holding him. Spoke to the woman in Clacton looking after her. We decided to tell her Morgan was away working. The woman wanted some money and I sent her some.'

'Money for what?'

'Food, clothes, rent, she said.' And to keep her mouth shut.

'I see.'

'Perhaps. But you still want to see straight lines where none exist. You still want to think you know what is and isn't real. You still think it matters to be able to make the distinction.'

25

Mitchell indicated to Laura where the mayor was sitting with his family and she went and sat beside him. He greeted her effusively and kissed her on the cheek. He searched around for the reporter, but the man had already gone. He introduced her to the others at his table. He offered to buy her a drink, which she declined. His hand rested on her arm. He explained to her that his wife had been unable to come because of illness. His daughter was there instead. 'It's her girl,' he said, meaning the winner of the beauty show.

The woman whose husband had died in Spain sat at the other side of the mayor, her hand resting next to his on the table. She was tanned, with heavy blue eye make-up. Her lips looked almost orange in the club lights; all her jewellery was yellow gold.

It was the mayor who had first approached Laura to let her know what had been suggested to him at a finance meeting he had recently attended. At the time she thought he was forewarning her of something, but later she realized that his supposedly confidential disclosures had been the opening gambit of the game into which they had all quickly entered. He had told her he was sympathetic, adamant that neither he nor his fellow councillors believed that she was in any way implicated in Mitchell's dealings. She understood then that she was being given a short-lived opportunity to betray Mitchell and save herself.

The comedian arrived on the stage above them. Everyone applauded the man. Mitchell had been against his inclusion in the night's events; his humour was a decade out of date. 'That's why he's so popular,' Laura had told him.

'Did Mitchell tell you we're holding an extraordinary meeting next week. First day back after the holidays. We all take this thing very seriously. Very seriously indeed.' He spoke without facing her.

'Of course you do,' she said. 'We all do. Very seriously.'

She waited for him to turn to her before looking up at the man on the stage.

'I hope he still intends to be present.'

'He'll be there.'

'You don't sound very certain. We've given him every opportunity. Me, personally, me, I've done all I can for him.'

'I'm sure he's very grateful.'

'I doubt that. There have been some who've accused me of being too lenient. Some think the police should have been involved.'

'I thought they were,' Laura said.

'Yes, well, officially-unofficially, if you know what I mean. No good letting these things get too far ahead of themselves.'

'Of course not. God forbid.'

'I'll be honest,' he said. 'It's a real mess.'

'I'm sure you've done everything you can,' Laura said, keeping him off his guard and uncertain.

He turned to the woman beside him. She lifted her empty glass to him and he immediately raised his arm for a waitress. Waitresses were not normally employed at the club, but tonight they had been hired to attend to the judges. The widow told the mayor that she didn't know what she'd do without him.

'I keep telling him,' she said to Laura. 'Keep telling him to come out to Spain. Leave here and come out there.'

'She does,' the mayor said.

'Especially now, now that . . .' She shook her head.

'I've told her,' the mayor said. 'Too much to do here. At least for now. But who knows, one day . . .'

'And is it anything serious, your wife?' Laura said. She looked beyond the man and saw Mitchell watching them from the bar. He raised his glass to her.

'She's just run down,' the mayor said.

'Still, it's good that the two of you are here, company for each other, a kind of unofficial escort, sorry, consort.' She turned to leave them, but the man caught her by her wrist.

'What's important,' he said, his voice a hiss, 'is that we get all this sorted out without too much fuss. We don't want everything blowing up in our faces now, do we?'

She leaned down to him and spoke close into his ear. 'What we want and what we get,' she said.

His grip on her tightened. 'I'd hoped it wasn't going to come to this,' he said.

'Liar,' Laura said softly, making the word appear as though she were licking her lips. 'Come to what?'

'You know what I'm talking about.'

She felt his grip slacken momentarily and she pulled her arm free, resisting the urge to rub where he had held her. The waitress arrived with their drinks.

The room grew much darker. Laura left the table and went to where Mitchell still stood at the bar.

Behind her, immediately following the departure of the comedian, the dancers came out on to the stage one at a time. Everyone applauded, and men whistled at them.

The red lights turned rapidly to blue and then back to red again as the six women finally assembled to begin their routine.

'What did he say?' Mitchell asked her.

'Nothing you wouldn't expect him to say.'

'Does he still think you should abandon the sinking ship?'

'He has no idea what you're planning.'

'Planning?' He lifted his glass to his mouth to avoid having to say more.

'Too slow,' she said. 'This is me, not him.'

'I'm not *planning* anything.'

'Of course you're not.' She turned back to watch the dancers on the stage. 'He expects you to turn up and take it like a man. He expects you to do the decent thing.'

'I know.'

'Is that what makes it all so easy?'

Five minutes later the dancers reached the end of their first sequence. They wore short pleated skirts and high boots. The skirts rose and spun with their every move-ment, and the pulsing lights hid their every imperfection, making them quicker, better co-ordinated.

'That's his daughter,' Laura said, indicating the woman beside the mayor.

'Big night all round, then,' Mitchell said, and he turned away from her to watch the barman empty the four tills of their early takings into coloured bags, after which he motioned for the man to hand them over to him.

26

The time before, it had been an overgrown verge in a lay-by twenty yards off the Great North Road.

Definitely a woman, definitely dead, and with signs of mutilation, but everything else still uncertain. Partially decomposed – the body was discovered in the middle of August; a family on their way to Scotland from Leicester for their annual holiday; this was where they always stopped; there was always a break here, space for the small children to stretch their legs, that sort of thing; dead – though nothing as yet confirmed – at least two months. Some decomposition, unclear what had already gone, where the darkened flesh became clothing, where the clothing had been removed.

The photographer has turned up. He sits in a car

beside his journalist companion, and together they watch a crowd form around a caravan, there to dispense tea and food.

The journalist is already writing in shorthand in his pad, imagining what the men inside the cordon can already see and he can't. The photographer is biding his time. His previous photograph was sold to several other newspapers in addition to being used on three occasions by his own. He is already considering how much more profitable his work might be were he to start operating as a freelance. He mixes with men who already make five times what he does and they encourage him to make the decision, to move out of the shallows into the depths.

'What do you think? Listen. "Interfered With" or "Tampered With" or "Molested"?' The journalist pressed his pencil into his chin, leaving a brief dimple.

'You don't know any of that yet.'

'Just keeping ahead of the game. There's a suspicion.'

There was always a suspicion, always an unattributable source.

No suggestion of the word 'Rape', even if the act itself had taken place.

'What else have you put?'

'Just the usual. Young woman. Identity unknown. Lonely, violent death. You ought to get over there, start pushing for a picture.'

But the photographer knew better than to try before the police had finished. He saw the frequent flashes of their own photographer working round the body and the surrounding verge.

A tall, untended hedge grew above where the body had been found; a litter-strewn ditch ran parallel to the road, between the body and the cars. The traffic in both directions slowed, but nothing was allowed to enter the lay-by. The man who owned the café in the caravan complained about the loss of his trade. The family from Leicester sat in their own car a short distance from the photographer.

'You ought to go and ask them about it,' he suggested to the journalist.

'What are they going to tell me? Stopped, got out, there she was. I can do that from here.'

'They might have seen if she was dressed or undressed, if her head had been smashed in.'

The journalist considers this for a moment and then leaves the car. ' "Our Holiday Horror",' he says.

The photographer watches him go. He knows how little, if anything, of the decomposed body he will be allowed to see. A canvas shelter has already been erected over the woman. The side of the caravan is clumsily painted with clouds and a pale blue sky.

There might be a clue in each blade of grass that has risen around the body. Dock leaves have grown and already started to die between the woman's legs.

Another month and who knows what might have been lost.

As he watches, he sees the men coming out of the

canvas structure batting away the flies from around their heads. Click. Some come out holding their hands over their mouths. Click, click.

A constable comes towards where he sits, then stops and is joined by another. The two men begin to erect a notice appealing for witnesses.

He might even be there, the photographer thinks, watching it all, assessing his chances, calculating the distances that have already begun to contract. They know it, too, he thinks, and he watches the two constables with the notice, one with a mallet held above his head, as they too look around them at the people gathered there. And seeing this, the photographer leans further out of the car and takes a photograph of the crowd, the pale line of rope stretching from one side of the picture to the other at waist height. In the finished picture it might look like a fault in the film and add appeal to the composition. Some of those gathered there realize what has happened and look towards him as he winds up his window.

The policeman with the mallet brings it down on the stake to which the notice is fixed and all attention is immediately refocused. Six blows and the notice is solidly planted.

An ambulance arrives and wails briefly to be let through the cordon. It has come for the body, and a murmur of expectation flows in its wake as people step back to let it through.

The journalist returns to the car. He seems pleased with what the family have told him.

'Didn't even recognize it for a body until they saw one of her legs. Thought it was just a bundle of rags somebody had dumped. And then the stink. Said it was alive with flies.'

He is happy that the body has remained undiscovered for so long. His speculative and lurid prose might now weave in and out of the putrefaction like ivy through a dying tree.

The ambulance passes them by and stops slightly ahead of them. It is still some way from where the body lies, but can get no closer because of the other vehicles already there. Two men climb down, walk to the rear, open the doors and pull out a stretcher, upon which lie a folded rubber bag, masks, rubber gauntlets and a coil of rope. They carry all this to the overgrown hedge. The men inside the cordon follow them; the crowd outside moves along the rope, this inviolable barrier, so they might get a better view of the body being brought out of its shelter.

The photographer leaves the car and walks only as far as the open doors of the empty ambulance. There is no one left to watch him. He climbs inside, where, surprised and pleased by how little of the sunlight penetrates, he quickly arranges a mound of blankets, then steps back, half closes one of the doors and takes several pictures. A large rubber ball attached to some breathing apparatus serves for the woman's head.

27

The earliest of the Kings Mitchell discovered was a sword-swallower. Ignatius Loyola King, born 1746, slid rapiers down the slender passage of his throat, performing outdoors on makeshift platforms in market places and anywhere else there was a crowd eager or gullible enough to pay for the chance to witness the walking tragedy and gasp of scarlet spout he might suddenly become before their very eyes.

In addition to the swords, Ignatius Loyola also worked in a travelling show with a bear. Mitchell knew all this because Ignatius wrote and published his own brief autobiography. The dealer in Cecil Court had shown it to Mitchell upon him making his enquiries concerning Morgan. The pamphlet was dated 1810, consisted of twenty-four pages, and had been printed in Cheapside.

Ignatius Loyola had four sons, all showmen, and had married twice. There was some suggestion that the death of his first wife was in some way connected with one of Ignatius's bears, but his own remarks on the matter remained tantalizingly obscure. He spoke throughout of his swords and other props as being genuine, of the finest shaved steel and alloy, but Mitchell understood all too well that this was part of the illusion, and that the swords were no more genuine than those he and Laura used.

Beginning his search, Mitchell believed that the closer he moved to the present, the better defined and more easily verifiable everything would become, but he had not properly understood then that the world of the Kings was governed by its own ever-changing laws and that it succumbed endlessly to reversals of nature and reason, where balances were created and lost and created anew solely according to need.

Even the name, he discovered, was victim to capricious whim. Until 1897 they had always been billed as 'The Mystical Kings', afterwards becoming 'Mythical' as a consequence of a printer's error.

Morgan was only two years old in 1897, learning to walk before he flew, and watching other children leading on the horses, playing urchin, throwing clubs to the jugglers and fanning knives for the throwers, serving their apprenticeships and awaiting their own entrances into that waiting world of worlds.

28

They resumed their questioning after a break. Tea had been served to them in enamel mugs. The detective in charge had arrived and come to join them. The two junior detectives behaved differently in his presence, keen to impress him. Morgan counted the sugar each man spooned into his cup. He himself had never had a sweet tooth.

'I loved my mother very much, as a matter of fact,' he said. This was in answer to a question put to him immediately before the short break and the arrival of the third detective. He assumed there was some suggestion that a bad relationship with his mother might have turned him into a hater of women. He had already sensed that the older detective did not share the others' enthusiasm for his guilt, and he wished there was some way he could confront the man directly with this understanding.

'She and my father worked a singing and comic act in the halls. Performed in a dozen places not two or three miles from where we are now. Coliseum, Alhambra, the Oxford on Oxford Street, North Woolwich Gardens, the Agricultural Hall in Islington, pantomimes at Covent Garden, the—'

He'd made his point.

'I performed first as a five-year-old dressed as a baby. All that was required of me was to cry on demand.'

During the break there had been a suspension of the rules. The stenographer had left them briefly. 'A call of nature,' he said, smiling at Morgan.

'Then try to keep your fingers still for a minute,' one of the detectives had said, causing all four men to laugh, even though the joke was clearly much used.

'Are we off the record now?' Morgan asked when the man had gone, and for an instant the two men thought he was about to confess something to them. 'No,' he said. 'Not that. Nothing so grand. I merely wondered about the technical and legal implications of the phrase itself – Off the Record – what it implied.'

'It implies nothing,' one told him.

'But you can still tell us,' the other added, but too quickly.

All three of them rose from their seats and paced around the small room.

'So you've been acting all your life?'

'If you mean am I acting now, then the answer—'

'No need. Wait until he gets back. We'll ask you again.'

Didn't all sons love their mothers? Didn't *they* love *their* mothers?

His mother had died of influenza, while he'd been in America. Her death had added to his sense of failure there. It should have been him, not Quinn, in that photograph with Arbuckle. *He* was the one who knew about dead mothers.

'Dead thirty-four years,' he said. 'And I still miss her. A day seldom passes when I don't think of her, when I am not in some small and seemingly insignificant way reminded of her.'

The stenographer returned, and with him came the detective in charge. He introduced himself.

'You wanted to say something about your train journey here,' the junior man said.

'I am obliged to tell you that your lodgings are at this very moment being searched,' the senior man said.

And the two of them looked at each other as though they had physically collided.

'Forget the train journey.'

'And have you found anything there to convince you of my guilt?' Morgan asked.

'I'm waiting to hear.'

'To hear what?'

'What, if anything, has been found. A Mr Quinn was present at—'

'Just as I said he would be.'

'Quite.'

'Anything you need to know, ask him.'

'Are you and he related, sir?'

Morgan regrets the use of the word. The façade had been slipping. 'Only very distantly. Hard to avoid it in my background.'

'I realize that.'

'I think you'll be disappointed.'

'Oh?'

'With what you find, what you won't find. I travel light, unencumbered. Again, the nature of my profession.'

'Tell me again about the scarf.'

'You know all that. I kept it.'

'Why?'

'Because it was—'

'What?'

'Attractive.'

'In what way?'

'It appealed to me.'

'In what way?'

'I'm an illusionist, a magician.'

'And?'

'All magicians have scarves. Scarves and doves.'

'You stole it.'

'All right, I stole it.'

'You killed her and then you stole it.'

'I stole it, that's all.'

'As a memento.'

'No.'

'Did you take something from each of the others?'

'I told you—'

'Something to add to your collection?'

'No.'

'We know what went missing each time. What was it, a shoe here, a bracelet there? You'd have quite a nice little collection by the time you'd finished.'

'You're wrong.'

'You still took them. It's a common enough trait. Some people just can't resist. Was that it? You always incriminate yourselves in the end. Always.'

In the corner, the stenographer coughed to attract their attention. Silence followed, broken only by the catching-up of his fingers.

'What about the train?' the senior detective asked his juniors.

The train on which Morgan had travelled from Southend back to London had been delayed for an hour because of a suicide on the track just beyond Dagenham.

'What will they say?' Morgan said. 'The newspapers? That she had everything to live for?'

How did he know it was a young woman? Someone on the train had heard from someone else who had spoken to the guard who had spoken to the driver.

'Strange,' Morgan said. 'Everything to live for, and yet she chose death. Why do you suppose that was?'

'Not our problem,' the senior detective said.

No, that's me. 'Do you think she waited unseen and then jumped from a bridge? Or do you think she might have stretched herself across the tracks and done it like that?' Like someone in a silent film. Like someone waiting to be rescued. Rescued by a man like—

'You seem very interested, concerned almost.'

The three detectives shared a glance.

—by a man like Roscoe Arbuckle.

'Very concerned.'

'I'm only human.'

Just think, just imagine, lying there and feeling the hum and tremor of those long metal lines at the train's approach. Imagine the rattle of the settling gravel between the sleepers. It was his guess that the young woman with everything to live for had chosen a spot close to the exit from a tunnel to throw herself in front of the engine, where she would not be seen, or where she might have been seen the instant before she was struck, but where the driver had not believed what he was seeing, still blinking against the sudden light and the body falling through it like a shadow, and unable to stop.

'Only human,' Morgan repeated. It was something he wanted clearly understood.

29

'Back to my story,' Quinn said.

But by then the story had become several stories, confusing in their connections and conflations, bleeding into each other, and where individual details might be appropriated or transposed with no real gain, no real loss.

Mitchell wanted to ask him why he was telling all this for the first time, what difference he believed it might make now that all the books were closed, all the accused and the accusers long since dead and buried.

'With the exception of you and me,' Quinn would have said, nodding slowly at some greater understanding. 'With the exception of you and me.'

'Do you have a picture of her?' Mitchell said.

'Why?' Like he was shielding himself from a blow.

'I wanted to see everything I could.'

'Nothing you haven't already seen.'

'Pictures of her when she was with Morgan, perhaps, something—'

'Something of her when she was with him on the ice cabinet in Blackpool? It was a one-night stand.' For Christ's sake. 'What did you expect, a full tour of the thing, twice nightly and matinées at weekends?'

'Then if it was such a big deal, such a one-off, he'd have made sure there were pictures. It's her I'm interested in, not him. I've seen all I want to see of him, and none of it—'

'You haven't seen anything. *I* saw *him*, me. Nobody else saw a thing. All anybody else saw was what he wanted them to see.'

'Including the police?'

'Of course including the police. They were as stupid as the rest of them. Who did they think they were dealing with? They had no idea. He could have told them anything he wanted and they'd have believed him.'

Mitchell doubted this. 'Not necessarily.'

'Listen to yourself.' He was shouting now. ' "Not necessarily." "Perhaps this, perhaps that." They were another audience to him, that's all. He worked them like he worked them all, took them one way and then another, up and down and round the houses. Where *he* wanted to go – *him*, not them.'

'Why would he do that if he had nothing to hide?'

'You tell me.'

No, you tell me. '*You* knew more than they did.' You and my mother. The thought had only then occurred to him. 'Did *she* believe he was innocent?'

'What did she know? She was—'

'Only a child?'

'She was a King.'

'One photograph, that's all I want to see.'

'I told you—' But there was the slightest flicker of his eyes towards the bedroom door. Skin after skin after skin.

Quinn stopped speaking. He sat back in his chair.

'What did you do?' Mitchell said after a minute of silence. The old man sat bathed in light. Dust drifted all around him in thick beams, like smoke.

'I burnt a small bag of things for him. I went to where he said it would be, took it away and burnt it.'

'What was in it?'

'I never knew.'

'Something that would have incriminated him?'

'He told me it was stuff from America. Film, photos, collector's stuff.'

'You never looked?'

'No, I never looked. If I'd looked, I would have known. I closed my eyes.'

And here I am, forty years later, forcing them open.

'You could at least have—'

'No, I couldn't. I was your age. I was you.'

'Me?'

'Why are you doing all this?'

'What do you mean you were me?'

'You're doing it because you want everything tied up with a neat red ribbon, everything sorted and understood and comfortably filed away, that's why you're doing it.'

'I wanted to know, that's all.'

'Like opening up a great big family album?'

'Something like that.'

'You're lying. You're not fooling anyone, least of all yourself. You're opening the book, taking a quick safe look inside, but most of all you want to slam it shut. You might want to know what's in there, but more than anything else you want to be able to say you looked and then you want to slam it shut and walk away from it all. Pity that wasn't an option open to the rest of us.'

'If you'd looked inside the bag before you burnt, and the thought also occurred to Mitchell that the bag hadn't been burnt, that it still existed somewhere and that only Quinn knew where, you'd have known for certain.' Slammed your own book shut.

'Perhaps. And perhaps I could have taken it straight to the police and claimed back your mother as my reward.'

'It might have been arranged.'

'I won't even laugh at that.'

'But you do have pictures of her when she was with Morgan.' He indicated the doorway. 'In there.'

A further minute passed before Quinn rose and went through into the room.

He came back with a photograph of Mitchell's mother as a girl, in one of her costumes, posing, silver-framed, polished, grinning, feathers and sequins, balanced on the toes of one foot, quality silver, her small cap, black where the metal had tarnished with age, the fingers of one hand splayed, polished through the plate in places, thumb and forefinger held together in a small, knowing *o* of the future.

It was all Mitchell could do to raise his hand and take it from the old man.

30

Laura went to the dressing room where the contestants were waiting. She needed to confirm that they had all arrived. The forms were being prepared for the judges. They were all there. All except for the winner, who had called earlier to say she would prepare herself at home and come later. And as she came, chauffeur-driven, rehearsing her speech of thanks and acceptance, her eyes would sparkle, blinding dots of light would flash across her perfect teeth, her hair would be the palest blond, and her seventeen-year-old lips would be the fullest, reddest, glossiest lips in the short, unhappy history of the contest. Laura wondered how many of the others saw all this as she knocked on the door and went in to them.

The girl who had come second to the Miss Television

Station winner last year sat with her legs above the level of her head. She said something about blood and colour as Laura edged round her. It was a cramped and uncomfortable room, still stale beneath its new bouquet of aromas. Outfits hung around the walls, most in their wrappers, and the whole scene was repeated in the mirrors in front of which the women sat.

The girl who'd come second said she wasn't happy. She said she'd written a month ago asking for a list of all the other entrants and that she hadn't received it. Hearing this, the others exchanged suspicious, accusatory glances, as though they believed the girl had somehow tried to gain an advantage over them. 'What?' the girl said, 'What?' as one by one they turned to look at her and openly assess her motives.

She had built a ziggurat of her four lilac cases with their white trim, one on top of the other, all perfectly aligned and centred.

It's because she knows she's going to come second again, Laura thought. She ignored the girl and asked if there was anything she could do for anyone else, if anyone had forgotten anything, if there was anything anyone really really needed. A girl at the far end of the room asked for some tissues. She held up an empty box. One of the others obliged. Laura wondered if any of them had yet seen the mayor's granddaughter. Of course they hadn't, it was the girl's first competition. The rest of them had started at the bottom, had paddled around and fallen over there; the mayor's granddaughter was going to start at the top – joke – and then bow out with her pride, trophy, crown, certificate, sash and modelling contract intact. None of them had the slightest idea of what they had all now become a part of.

All Mitchell's doves, she thought, all preening and fluttering and diverting attention from whatever sleight of hand he was at that very moment practising alone.

The girl who had asked for the tissues screamed and shook her hands, complaining that her nail varnish was refusing to dry correctly.

Stop complaining, Laura thought. You paint your nails, they chop Mitchell's hands off. You draw a line under your eye and then draw it again because it is infinitesimally less than perfect, and they gouge his eyes out. You carry on like those stupid show birds, and they wring Mitchell's neck.

'It's in the regulations,' the girl who had come second last year said. 'If any contestant requires to see a list of the other contestants, then that list shall be supplied free of charge no later than seventy-two hours prior to midday on the day of the competition.' Her pretence at quoting did not fool Laura. 'It's in the rules.'

'Sorry,' Laura said. 'Perhaps the Christmas mail.'

'Seventy-two hours.' As though this closing emphasis added some substance to her useless appeal.

31

That Morgan's death was a bloody and terrible tragedy –
involving, as it did, the common ingredients of every
tragedy – there can be no doubt; it was a safe, predictable,
almost reassuring thing to say. That, as others had
claimed, it was avoidable, Mitchell was less certain. There
had been a time when he might have gone further and
said that not only was it unavoidable, but that it was
in fact planned, that Morgan knew precisely what he
was doing as he made all his preparations, that he knew
it and understood it better than anyone – and certainly
better than any of the other Kings, most of them
still stumbling around, heads down, blinking and rubbing
their eyes against the glare of outrage and mistaking it for
the brilliant sun of fame – that he understood what was

happening to him even as the life was being crushed from him, as he and his last grand illusion became both immovable object and irresistible force, as the creak of the swaying trunk and lifting roots became the thrashing of branches and leaves on their way to the ground.

Morgan, Mitchell knew, could no more have severed himself from the Kings than he could have severed his own arm. But even he, Mitchell also knew, must have had the sense every now and then to peer through the curtains into the watching world, and to take note of the boredom and distaste curdling its amusement to scepticism, its disbelief to indifference and finally revulsion.

Perhaps, Mitchell once considered, Morgan was seduced in the same way he was later seduced; but perhaps for Morgan the options, the ways ahead, were neither so tempting nor so clearly defined. How were ten generations of acrobats or bareback riders suddenly going to produce a clerk or a factory foreman?

32

'You'll be pleased to hear we've completed our search.'

Forty-eight hours had passed. The junior detective pushed himself back from the table and the noise of his scraping chair filled the room.

'Why pleased?' Morgan said.

'Turn of phrase. We're very thorough. Nothing escapes us.'

Not even an escapologist? Morgan shared a knowing glance with the senior detective. 'No, nothing escapes you,' he said.

'Mr Quinn says he has no idea where you were on the evening in question.'

'I already told you that.'

'In fact he says he hadn't seen you for three or four

days prior to the evening in question.'

'It might have been nearer a week. We come and go.'

'The nature of your work. Yes, you said.'

The senior detective remained silent throughout all this, and it occurred to Morgan to wonder if the man, knowing what he did, and having been through all this a dozen times before, was not already convinced of his innocence and was now merely letting his juniors go through this blade-sharpening exercise.

For his part, the senior detective was considering how best to ask Morgan if he knew how far it was, as the crow flew, from that lay-by on the Great North Road to the Grand Theatre in Leeds, where, he had already ascertained, Morgan had been appearing in May and June of the year in question. He offered Morgan another of his endless cigarettes. 'Where were you last August?' he said, his flaring match at that instant only inches from Morgan's eyes.

'Last August? August? Summer. Touring, probably. Definitely. Touring.'

'August the seventeenth. Saturday.'

It is clear to Morgan that the man already knows the answer. 'I've no idea.' He drew deeply on the cigarette, tipped back his head and blew smoke to the low ceiling, watching as it spread in a circle, thickened by the light there.

'You were in Poole.'

'Poole, Poole, Poole. Yes, I was. Two weeks. The Hippodrome, Boscombe. Seaside show. And?'

'There from August the second to the twenty-fifth.'

'Known in the trade as a triple-ender. Three weekends, three lots of holidaymakers. Why?'

'You tell us,' one of the younger detectives said.

'Branksome Dene Chine,' the senior man said.

'What?'

'Branksome Dene Chine.'

'Is that a man?'

'A place. And, please, don't disappoint us by saying you've never heard of Branksome Dene Chine. Everyone who goes on holiday there knows of Branksome Dene Chine.'

'It rings a bell,' Morgan said.

'I'm sure it does. Nevertheless, it needn't concern us here. Not yet.'

It rang a bell, and Morgan alone heard the long slow tolling of it.

33

There was Jacob 'Jaybird' King, perhaps a grandson of Ignatius Loyola, who made his living in a succession of circuses as a lion-tamer, famed for being one of the first men to put his head inside the creatures' mouths.

'Glorious' Gloria King – in reality Dorothy (Mitchell's mother's first name) – the earliest of the King women to promote herself to the first rank. She started life as a fortune-teller, trained for the high wire, and then perfected her act of falling from a raised platform with her ankles bound by a cord which pulled her up short only a few feet from the ground, her cry of pain at the jolt with which she was stopped drowned by the screams of the audience tricked into thinking she had lost her grip on the trapeze and fallen.

'Starving' Charlie King – father of the Cut-Price Cannonball – who began by blowing flames and then moved on to eating broken glass, nails and coins, until eventually there was little he was unable to consume if the circumstances and inducement demanded it.

Mitchell found Moses King in a book on Victorian table-rappers, perhaps the best known of all the Kings before Morgan. Moses ran his own Spiritual Lyceum in Putney, in addition to which he toured the provincial halls and institutes as well as holding private seances to offer advice and comfort from the dead to whoever wanted to hear it.

He was exposed as a fraud in 1891, and after that he dropped out of sight. He resurfaced in 1903 as a music-hall comedian and then as a bone-breaker. He, too, worked with a girl assistant, repeating and establishing the pattern. All Mitchell knew of this girl was her name – Lilly Dawson. Lilly, he knew, had been his mother's mother's name, but had not been passed on. He searched for Lilly Dawson, following Moses into the maze and losing him there. Much later, having convinced himself that the girl was one of those peripheral, ever-moving relatives of his mother's, he discovered that the name was also the title of a popular novel of the time about spiritualism – one Moses had most likely read and then appropriated to christen her, perhaps out of a sense of regret or affection for his former life, or perhaps in scorn for the audience which had driven him from that easy and profitable existence into his damaging shows of strength.

Mitchell was gratified – just as he had been reassured to read of Ignatius and his swords – to discover that one of Moses' most impressive acts had been to batter a foot-square block of ice into pieces with his forehead.

It did not matter to Mitchell that Morgan may never have known Moses, or seen his act as a boy; it did not matter that this sudden turn in the trail looped away from Houdini in New York and back into the alleyways and passages of the East End where the ageing Moses acquired his second, short-lived fame. What mattered was that here, amid all those other deceits and conceal-ments, was an undeniable bond, no less strong for being based only on supposition and the undeniable need to make connections, and no more likely to weaken and break merely because it existed solely in the mind of the man who had made the connection in the first place.

Mitchell had returned to the dealer in Cecil Court and inquired about the novel *Lilly Dawson*. Of course the man had heard of it. He didn't have a copy in stock, but would look for one. He consulted the catalogues of other dealers, but could not find one. He quoted Mitchell a price. Mitchell left a deposit and his address. He waited for three months, but there was nothing from the man. Mitchell changed his address. If the dealer had found the book and tried to contact him, then he had known nothing of it, and in time he had even forgotten the name of the book's author.

34

Is It Possible – Is It Humanly Possible? – that one of these women was killed in a crowded cinema? Is It Possible – How, In God's Name? – that both she and her killer were in the same audience and that they were the last two people to hear out the national anthem in its entirety? What kind of clue is that so short a way into a new reign?

Found by a cleaner pushing her brush at eleven o'clock the following morning, the cinema's dawn. Thought she was a coat, bundled up, pushed down and forgotten.

The pursuit begins anew. A simple matter of interviewing the six hundred members of the same audience. How fast would a guilty fish have to swim to avoid a net trawled as slowly as that one?

All About Eve, starring Bette Davis. Misleadingly lurid

posters still on the boards when the police left and the press arrived.

Kathleen Rachel Mary Docherty.

VICIOUS SLAYING OF MOTHER-TO-BE.

Vicious Slaying Of Unmarried Mother-To-Be.

Cause of death: puncture of the heart by a long, sharp instrument. If it was a knife, then it was longer and thinner than usual. Twice. No scream heard. (And no, the killer hadn't chosen the film and known when a communal scream of excited fear might drown out Kathleen Rachel Mary Docherty's own. So, presumably, the first insertion of the long slender blade had done its job.)

And how long had she known? Three months, the pathologist reckoned. Not much chance of her not having known.

The photographer composes his picture to include Bette Davis. Fifty yards down the road stands a news-paper vendor's placard declaring the murder. He con-siders borrowing the board and positioning it beneath the poster, but then decides against this as being too contrived.

He has turned freelance and is becoming more selec-tive, less obvious, more aware of his various markets, more professional. He has visited this same cinema himself. People passing by in the street pause to watch him. It is still winter, not yet spring, and he has recourse to his flashgun even at noon. He takes a dozen shots, a mosaic of the whole building.

Having chosen his position carefully, he afterwards discovers that his own image is reflected in one of the glass panels beside the cinema entrance, and that a woman in a strapless dress is leaning seductively backwards into his arms with her eyes full of longing. Another woman stands inside the cinema and looks out at him. It might even be the ghost of the three-month-pregnant murdered girl.

He convinces himself that his new-found professionalism is already paying dividends, already satisfying a need he had previously scarcely been aware of.

35

In March of that fatal year, a member of the audience at a touring circus had been injured by Benjamin 'Bull's-Eye' King, knife-thrower and brother to the Cannonball, having rushed from her seat to spread her arms and legs inside his target. It was always women who came, and their eagerness was seldom wasted on Benjamin and his brothers.

The wound was only superficial – inner thigh just above the knee (no more to the Kings than a bruised thumb to a carpenter) – but was deemed sufficient in that time of cold winds for a formal inquiry to be held, and for Benjamin afterwards to be expediently sacked from the circus.

Mitchell searched the reports of each of these Stations

of the Cross in the hope that his mother might somehow be involved, or if not involved, then appear fleetingly as a witness. But she had had no part in the circus, and was working at the time with two of her mother's sisters at the Theatre Royal in Nottingham in a minstrel review. There was a photograph of her taken a year previously, wearing a straw boater, her face black, her mouth and eyes ringed white. She might have come across Benjamin during those hard, dismantling years, but she had never worked with him.

The more he saw, the more that came to light, so the more Mitchell wished he had known earlier of this hidden history, of all this disguise and name-changing and flitting from shadow into light and back again.

Mitchell's father had been a clerk in the civil service, proud of his occupation, proud of his employer, and he rose by degrees, his slow promotion guaranteed by his obedient reliability. After his mother's life with the Kings, and particularly after Morgan's death, it was easy for Mitchell to understand the man's appeal. Opposites had attracted. The engagement lasted only eight weeks. It was a register-office wedding, to which none of the Kings were invited.

He saved her. He saved her from the Kings and he saved her from herself and it was something she would do well never to forget. He was fourteen years older than her and he always looked and behaved a decade older than he was. He was injured during the war when an un-discovered bomb exploded as he made his way along the

Embankment to his office. Afterwards, he walked with a proud limp, and was even better respected and trusted by the safe, dull people with whom he worked. In the following seven years he gained promotions for which another man might have had to wait ten years.

36

It was time for the sword cabinet. No-one wanted it. It merely added to the advertised list of the evening's entertainments. It was New Year's Eve.

'It's all about not wanting to be the people you actually become,' Laura had said upon first seeing the ballroom.

'More straightforward than that,' Mitchell had said. 'Drink, big ideas, sex.'

She hadn't said anything to him at the time, but this facing-up, this reluctant journey from the necessary fictions of life into its unavoidable realities had been the first of her true resentments. Finding Mitchell with one of the prospective beauty queens a year later had seemed almost nothing by comparison. Both Mitchell and the woman were drunk. He accused Laura of overreacting. A barrage of argument and recrimination followed. Laura argued and fought within the confines of her loss and her regret. The woman hadn't even come third, had only been Highly Commended. Who, she remembered shouting at Mitchell, who, who with even an ounce of self-respect, would do that, with him, on a promise of being only a Highly Commended?

Ladies and Gentlemen. Pause. Ladies and Gentlemen, I give you, for your further entertainment, your excitement and your delight, Mitchell and Laura. Mitchell and Laura and the Sword Cabinet. Lost Magicals and Lovelies, misplaced Mighties and Unforgettables. Mitchell and Laura. Mitchell and Laura. Another switch flicked, another sequence of lights. The pop of a microphone being switched off.

Mitchell and Laura went out on to the stage from opposite sides. A quarter of the audience applauded. One of the barmen pushed the wheeled cabinet out behind Mitchell. The hush of anticipation at its appearance was shallow and brief.

Flourishes. Spins. The flash of reflected light.

Mitchell and Laura. Here To Amaze. Before Your Very Eyes. Thank You, Thank You. I Thank You.

Mitchell turned the cabinet from side to side and showed everyone its innards. He opened and closed the two halves of its door. Upper open and closed, then lower, lower then upper.

Everyone watching him knew that he had disgraced himself. It was why most of them were there, all coming now out of today's shadows and raising their previously hushed voices; all staring where they had once done the decent thing and looked away.

Laura moved around the cabinet in the opposite direction to him. She saw beyond the glare of the coloured lights to those large parts of the room where no-one paid them the slightest attention.

The barman returned with the bag of Mitchell's swords, dropping it several feet short of where Mitchell had told him. Mitchell retrieved the bag, opened it on his knee and drew the thirteen polished blades out into the light and rattled them together.

'What they want,' Laura said to him through her grin, 'is to see you chop your head off.'

'Perhaps I ought to. Perhaps I might. Save them the job.' He fanned the blades and waved them in a figure of eight as though they were giant fingers.

'Don't,' she said, not knowing why she said it, and surprising them both.

Mitchell looked at her. The tips of the shining swords rested on the stage at his feet.

'If you say so.'

She felt as close to him then as she had felt in a year. There were limits to most people's loss – an equation of expectation over weakness – but not to Mitchell's. He had once tried to explain to her the difference between what was referred to as so-called respectable failure and the failure that might come at a man out of the blue like a car on a night road. She hadn't properly understood him then and she didn't want to try to understand him now. She found herself wondering if he didn't in some way take pleasure in his failure. She wondered if one man might be motivated by failure just as another might be motivated by his dream of success.

'More leg,' he said to her.

She came back to the front of the cabinet and raised one leg against the lower door. The glitter in her tights caught the light. Someone in the audience whistled at her. She lifted her leg higher, turned it out at an angle to the cabinet and twisted her foot from side to side. A seven-year-old girl at ballet lessons. She smiled to herself at the sudden memory.

Mitchell was talking now, starting his routine.

She smiled down at the mayor and the painted widow sitting beside him. Only the mayor looked back up at the stage. Others around the table made no effort to lower their voices. The rest of the judges were already in place. People came and went in faceless shapes across the dance floor, caught in the gloom and the spinning lights, and making them look as though they were walking on the bottom of an ocean. Mitchell had to shout louder to make himself heard above the resurgent noise, and Laura wished he could have been spared at least that smallest of indignities.

37

'You won't believe this, but that talking donkey went on to do three more ads. It became a celebrity. They only used my voice on the first of them. No agent. I did the one for a petrol company.' Quinn put on the voice of the donkey. ' "Only an ass would say no to Such-and-Such gas." The fat man was long finished by then. I taught that donkey everything it knew. Imagine that – kicked in the balls by a talking donkey.'

It was early evening by then, and the falling sun shone even more vividly into the upper half of the room. Mitchell smelt woodsmoke. Children shouted in the street outside.

Quinn sat in silence for several minutes.

'Did the police ever come back to you?' Mitchell asked him.

'Only the once. The first time they only had a warrant to search. The second time they wanted to take things away, pieces of Morgan's clothing, stuff they found among his cases.'

'Something to connect him to the later crimes?'

'That's what they thought. But there was nothing there that was going to do that.'

'Meaning if there was anything you didn't burn then it was somewhere else.'

'In his rooms in Clacton, where your mother sat waiting for him.'

Mitchell was now more convinced than ever that Quinn believed Morgan was involved, if not in all, then at least in one of the killings.

'First place we rented in Los Angeles, a single room with a washbasin, looked out on to a courtyard with orange trees growing in it. One night, Morgan went out and stripped one of those trees of every piece of fruit it held. We ate ten oranges a day for a week until we started to turn yellow. There must have been three or four hundred of them. The rest we hid in a sack in the basement. He had some idea of selling them, but never did. They started to rot and pull in flies. After that he took them out and dumped them. That was Morgan – all or nothing.'

'Did *you* visit my mother while they held him?'

'Of course I did. When it was safe to go. I took

money to the woman she was with. To tell you the truth, I wished your mother and the woman could have stayed together. It didn't seem right – not after his arrest, the things they alleged – her and Morgan being together. She was still only, what, twelve or thirteen, but you could already see what she was shaping up to look like.'

'Couldn't she at least have come back here to you while he was being interviewed?'

'Morgan wanted her kept as far away as possible from anything connected to him. They were still convinced he was their man.'

'I doubt that,' Mitchell said.

'If they weren't, they never let on.'

'Perhaps.'

'What makes you think they weren't serious about charging him?'

'Nothing. The transcript of his interview.'

'Never knew that kind of stuff was made public.'

'Just everything I've read since,' Mitchell said. 'Tell me more about Roscoe Arbuckle.'

'Nothing to tell. That was it. Morgan got left behind at the graveside and I got to travel with the man in his Pierce Arrow with its built-in bar and toilet all the way to the Wilshire Hotel where the whole world was waiting for him. Not to hear Morgan tell it, of course. According to Morgan, it was *him* in the car, him and Arbuckle, big friends. It was another of those chances he couldn't not take. About a year afterwards he got a job working as a props man for a company that turned out stag films. That was the name of the company, Stag Films.'

'And you think Morgan's connection with Arbuckle, however brief or illusory, and what happened afterwards, helped him get the job?'

'Who knows?'

'But he made more of it than it warranted?'

'Later, he was the star of some of those films. Real stud. To be honest, all the lying, it didn't hurt him; he made a few friends on the strength of it, some of them pulled a few strings for him. One of the films they made starred this obese man and three or four much younger women, all a bit obvious. I fell out with him over that. Not thick enough skinned, I suppose.'

And you never trusted him afterwards, Mitchell thought. And that was why, all those years later, you weren't surprised by his involvement in the murders and why you burnt the bag. You did what you did for my mother, and not for him.

'Morgan could have left a trunk of his belongings in any one of a dozen places,' Mitchell said.

'More like twice that.'

'How long overall did they hold him?'

'Don't ask me questions you already know the answers to.'

Mitchell nodded his apology.

' "Five meals a day she gave me. God rest her soul. Fat as a pig by the time I was your age, all pink and shining and pumped up ready to burst." I'd seen him on the screen, forever chasing those young women, them kissing his powdered cheeks and trying to get their arms round him. If he was a joke, then at least he knew it and made it work for him.'

Unlike Morgan.

'He told me something on that trip in his car. He told me that Fate was just as cruel to those people it forgot entirely as to those it remembered badly. It didn't make any sense at the time.'

'But it does now?' It was only after he'd asked that Mitchell realized Quinn was talking about himself.

'Work it out,' Quinn said, and for the first time since they had started talking four hours earlier, there was something approaching hostility in his voice, something distilled and still potent at the centre of all that remained intact.

'He took out a bottle from that built-in bar and drank from it. I thought he was going to offer it to me, but he didn't. He told me to go on waving. I began to feel famous. I felt more famous then than I ever felt as the voice of the donkey. What a measure of a life.'

38

MAN HELD. Better: SUSPECT HELD. POLICE QUIZ MAN. IS THIS THE FACE OF A KILLER?

And this is how it once was, still is for that matter: look, see for yourself.

A seven-year-old boy, two years into the century, indistinguishable from a smiling, long-haired girl. Remarks turning sour about the mother always having wanted a girl but only getting the one son, and then, after all that, the facts of life resolving themselves with the photographs of these women.

A mother in a silver leotard and plumed headdress with a child, naked, poised on her knee. A smiling, retouched face, teeth whitened, hair blackened, ten years out of date, casually signed With All Best Wishes in white ink across one corner, a wide border to allow for framing, matinée idol that never was.

The stenographer remains a measure of all their silence, the tap of his finger the beeping of a machine attached to a man's heart.

Morgan wishes they had not put the picture of his mother, of his mother with him, on the table next to the pictures of all those dead women.

Remarks are made – smirks exchanged – about the difference between the publicity photograph and the face of the man at the table. The same photograph, as he has already been told, that was found among the possessions of the most recently killed of the women.

A new picture will need to be taken. For their files. Less flattering. Routine procedure in enquiries like this.

And Morgan understands better than any of them, that just as one cannot avoid the transformation of the guile-less and the innocent by fixing their own final and unalterable poses, so his own words and actions can now never be retrieved.

And along with those pictures of himself and his mother is one of the pair of them, his father standing apart, amid the ranks of the Kings in their heyday, eighty, a hundred confident smiles, flexed muscles, struck poses, and scattered at their feet like the trophies of a shooting party, their bag of clubs, balls, chains, knives and swords. And to the far left of the photograph the blur of uncatchable flame spouting from the mouth of a fire-eater, the name of whom Morgan has forgotten, and which he tries hard to remember, to cement in place the foundations of the past before turning once again to the crumbling masonry and falling tiles of the present and the future.

39

In his father's hands the Kings became something to be ridiculed and despised, something to be waved at Mitchell – and anyone else who ever came close to his mother – as a red flag of warning. Everything about them and the lives they led became suspect, beneath contempt. She seldom spoke of them, except when she and Mitchell were alone, and then her reminiscences were abruptly halted when the taste in her mouth became either too bitter or too sweet to go on. If she savoured any fondness for her childhood in their midst, for her life with Morgan and Quinn, then she kept it buried deep.

To Mitchell's father, there was nothing in any of the Kings, Morgan in particular, which did not afterwards point to a flaw or weakness in her own character. He attacked her as a stonemason might attack an untouched slab, aware only vaguely of the hidden beauty and value of the form waiting to be revealed by his work. But he struck her too long and too hard, uncertain of that hidden design, until eventually she lay reduced and with no solid core of confidence or faith from which to build herself anew.

In Mitchell's eyes, the man grew deformed by his bitterness, indignant that his wife did not continually express her gratitude to him for having saved her.

After the night in Blackpool and Morgan's crushed and frozen corpse, she had run and continued running until she was too exhausted to go on. She had been a girl of barely fifteen on that May night, and a woman of twenty when she met and married her husband. Without him, he told her often enough, she would still be on her knees, exhausted and waiting to be helped up.

Search as hard as he might, Mitchell found nothing of those lost five years, merely the echoes of Morgan's death fading forward and the life of his father retold endlessly into the past, as though the history of one life was doing the work of two.

As a child, Mitchell was threatened with the prospect of the Kings coming to reclaim him, there being nothing his mother would afterwards be able to do to get him back from them. The threat became the rotten seed of a decade of nightmares.

He had tracked down others before coming to Quinn. He never explained who he was or why he wanted to know about Morgan, and about his assistant in particular. He told most he was a journalist with an interest in the variety halls. Their own descendants were still being born. Few were able or willing to tell him anything new; some refused even to speak to him; and still not even the feeblest of light was shone into the darkness of those missing years.

He spoke to the son of the Cannonball. The man – a mechanic at a bus depot – was at first reluctant to say anything, but when he was finally induced to talk, he spoke of his father as though he were no more than a distant cousin, and certainly not someone who had any direct or relevant bearing on himself. Mitchell made no reference to the film of the fatal flight.

Others had heard of Morgan, but few had any recollection of Mitchell's mother. They showed him their own photographs, which he searched assiduously.

Most of what he saw and heard only confirmed what he already knew – that speculation had buried the Kings and accusation had planted their headstone.

He visited 'Marvello Memory Man' King, then eighty-four and sitting in a nursing home. The man had made his living by memorizing every football player and every game played in every league in the country since the turn of the century. The assistant who took Mitchell to him warned him not to expect too much. Marvello – he still insisted on being called the ridiculous name twenty years after his last performance – retained all those footballing details, but apart from these and the tethering post of his own name, everything else in the world was a spreading oblivion to him.

Mitchell spent an hour with him, during which time the man never stopped reciting. Even while drinking tea he went on talking, the liquid dribbling from his lips. It was how Mitchell believed he would eventually find Quinn.

40 _____

The photographer pulls the sheets from his bed. The cinema remains pinned to the nearby wall. He can lie back on his mattress and look at it. The Killer Has Been Caught. He knows how much everyone wants to believe this. In the world outside, a general election is being held. Soon they may even abolish the death penalty. There has already been talk. The Killer May Have Been Caught.

The face of the man looks back at him, surprise in his eyes, cut in half by the thin white line of the restraining rope.

The reports redefine and confuse themselves. He has spent two unprofitable days outside the police station waiting for another picture of the man. He has spoken to the reporter and he has scoffed at the police search.

Anything can be hidden and never found. There is talk of the man now being questioned having lived with a young girl, his daughter perhaps. Why would a man appearing twice daily in Southend still have lodgings in London and waste all that money on travelling? The woman in the cinema poster still has her watching ghost.

His own sister had been killed when she was only four years old, struck by a car as she played in the street, and then carried into the house by the driver who sobbed so convulsively that he looked ready to drop her at every step. Two years later, the house in which he had lived, and the street in which the house stood, had been obliterated by bombs. And a month after that, the graveyard in which his sister lay buried was bombed and cratered and this time the dead and not the living were blown to pieces. He had not attended the reburial service with his mother.

He had collated the facts: a bedsit, a bomb site, a lay-by, a cinema, beside the seaside, beside the sea.

It occurs to him that someone ought to conduct a survey of all the women's bodies found on all the bomb sites in the years since the bombs and rockets had stopped falling. He supposes that the killers believed in the hundreds of others buried in the raids and never found, but he knows this to be a myth, knows that everyone, dead and alive, and his own twice-destroyed sister, was accounted for.

Today, instead of returning to the police station to continue his useless vigil, he will visit some of the sites overgrown with willowherb and still mounded with rubble, and photograph them instead. It might one day be just as important to know about the scene of the crime before the crime was committed there as it was to know about it afterwards. He knows this is a perverse breed of logic, but he believes it to be well suited to the times.

And soon, preferably before the man's release, he will go to Southend, to the theatre there, and take some more photographs.

On the floor beside his bed, amid all his other magazines scattered there, is a photography magazine in which is advertised a device which allows pictures to be taken round corners using an improbable-looking horizontal periscope, and the boldest claim made for this unlikely device is that a man looking round a corner in advance of arriving there is a man looking into the future.

This Newspaper Supports The Death Penalty.

It Is The View Of This Newspaper . . .

The stories of the man's imagined atrocities might now be embellished upon by the ordinary facts and details of his life and forged anew in a common currency. There is – thankfully – no mention yet of a war record, and the country is still in love with its heroes. Besides which, the man is clearly too old to have served in the armed forces. No, no adjustments will need to be made on that score.

The photographer's hand slides over the retouched bodies of the smiling women in search of his laughable promise of the future.

41

Laura climbed inside the cabinet and swung open the upper door. She waved to the people below and cursed them through her smile. The top of the box was only inches above her head. It smelt stale. She positioned herself. She lowered her arms and checked that all the entry slots were clear and that the sword tips at their exit holes were ready for her to release them. Some of these, the upper ones, she operated by hand; the others were connected to small pedals in the base of the cabinet. Mitchell's retractable blades would slide telescopically back into their handles the moment they were fitted into the slots and pushed. By judging the passage of the blades 'through' her and the box, pressing the correct sequence of pedals would ensure that the corresponding tips appeared at the far side. She had long since stopped trying to understand how anyone was taken in by the illusion, and wondered instead what it truly was they came to see.

Outside, Mitchell shouted louder. He closed the upper door, sliding open the oval hatch which would keep her face visible.

A badly positioned spotlight shone into her eyes, dazzling her and preventing her from looking anywhere but down at the audience below. Light entered the cabinet along all its joints and came through the waiting slits like the swords themselves.

Although enclosed, she was aware of Mitchell moving around her. He came between her and the light, darkening the interior. She could hear clearly everything he said, see most of what he did, feel his hands slapped frequently on the side of the box.

He rattled his swords. One of them was the genuine article. He would hand this down to someone in the audience to inspect. Tonight he handed it to the mayor. She watched him climb down from the stage and slash the air beside the man's head. On other nights, Mitchell would produce a carrot from his pocket and cut it in slices. This blade would pass behind her, further back in the box than it appeared from below, coming in at an angle into a sheath attached to the backboard. The corresponding tip would emerge several inches forward of this.

The mayor rose at Mitchell's approach, and at first

looked as though he was about to defend himself, but then Mitchell said something and everyone else at the table laughed and the man sat back down. Mitchell gave him the sword to inspect.

Waiting for him to come back to her, Laura looked to the side of the stage, where some of the beauty contestants had gathered to watch. Most were now ready for the competition, due to begin after the swords. All of them wore their coats. She did not want to be seen by them like this. Elsewhere in the club she had some authority over them. Now they needed nothing from her. She wondered if the mayor's granddaughter was among them yet, but guessed without searching that she would not be, that she would be somewhere else, somewhere warm and safe, clean and familiar, and the girl would be kept for ever young and beautiful, uncontaminated, that she would grow into her mother, and having been her mother, she would then turn into the wealthy widow with her hand resting on the mayor's arm.

Mitchell returned to the stage.

It was time to begin.

He gave her the signal that the first sword was ready.

She saw him come closer, heard the click as this one true blade found its place, and then the scraping sound it made as it slid into its sheath behind her. She remembered to stop smiling for a moment, look surprised and pained, and then resume smiling. The applause was louder than she had anticipated.

42

The centre no longer held. Not in Mitchell's mind, in his reconstruction of the interview and its peripheral chapters growing too much flesh and history of their own; not in Morgan's mind, where his own confused motives were unravelling too quickly ahead of him and where the mask and the face were turning all too easily one into the other; and certainly not in the mind of the man in charge of the operation, who saw more clearly than any of them that not enough had been found, that too much remained hidden and missing. He was convinced of Morgan's involvement – he would put it no more force-fully than that – in the killing of the woman six days previously, but everything else remained too circumstantial. Too much was happening. Details of all the other killings were coming at him too quickly and from too many directions.

Maureen Elizabeth Marshall, Miss, found in Branksome Dene Chine, Poole, famous beauty spot. Gets about a bit, always did, that kind of girl, friendly sort, very independent for her age, bit flirty, but very nice with it. A beauty spot of which the popular seaside resort could be rightly proud. As far as anyone could remember, she had never said boo to a goose. Visited by tens of thousands every summer. And now this.

Gagged and bound and killed by having her throat cut above the larynx. Breasts slashed with a knife, one nipple bitten off. Body open from groin to breastbone. Partially hidden.

Someone, somewhere, has spotted a clue. Eileen, Kathleen, Doreen, Maureen. Double *e* times four. But these are the clues they put up like disturbed birds and then manage to catch only the flightless.

But, Jesus Christ, dear Godalbloodymighty, what kind of man would do that to a woman, Jesus Christ, dear God Almighty?

'It may be necessary,' the man in charge of the operation says, 'to take an impression of your teeth.'

'I see.'

'And your dentist is who?'

There are several dentists.

Distant inquiries are already being made. He knows that.

One of the two junior detectives, now relegated to

mostly silence, thinks of his own young wife's nipples and then traces them up to her smiling face. He tries to imagine what it would take to bite off even the smallest part of her.

Did any of them know of the Tollard Royal Hotel?

What of it?

Considered in its day to be the finest hotel in the resort, some said in the whole of Dorset.

What about it?

Maureen Elizabeth Marshall, Miss, had worked part-time in the kitchen of the Tollard Royal Hotel. Another one of those clues up and flapping vigorously out of reach.

Last seen at eleven-fifteen the night before her body was discovered.

'And your performance at the Boscombe Hippodrome ended at what time?'

'Seaside show. Early-to-bed audiences. Sea air.'

'What time?'

'The show at ten. My own personal part in it shortly after nine.'

'You weren't the main attraction, then?' one of the junior men says.

But, surely, the more they found (or didn't find), the fewer direct connections would remain. An unspoken thought. Only a favour from an old agent had secured him his work in the show. He knew even then that something far more impressive was needed if he was ever to regain any of his former glory.

'Give you a bit of a thrill, does it, all this? Get a kick out of it?'

'What was it, escapologist again?'

Bound, gagged, blindfolded, chained, boxed, locked, cast into darkness.

Oh, you'd be surprised how much can be achieved by the simple expedient of a trapdoor.

They study his face for some indication of the unspoken thought. A line of sweat has formed running down his left temple.

'Warm in here.'

'Not really.'

'No, not the main attraction. An old-time variety hall show.'

Dull nostalgia, smoke of familiarity, fire of involvement.

'Must get to you a bit, that. Not being the centre of attraction and everything. Especially after everything you've done in the past.'

'Not really.'

'It would get to me.'

'I dare say.'

'Not even after all those films?'

'A long time ago.'

'Tell me which ones, I might have seen them, might have seen you.'

He doubts it.

The boy who worked the trapdoor at the Boscombe Hippodrome was worse than useless. He would find someone new. As though the decision still rested with him. Pluck another flower from the nursery of waiting Kings.

'Go on, tell me – what films?'

But even he cannot remember their titles. Strange, that. After all that time they were gone from him like beads off a broken string.

43

Mitchell still had a partial transcript of the inquiry into Morgan's death. He found it in the first of the chests he opened, beneath a protective layer of newspaper, sitting squarely and unmissably on top of everything else that had been packed away there.

It was in this same case that he found the small silver skullcap to which a pair of pointed emerald-green ears had been sewn, covered over its entire surface with sequins which it shed in a dry scale as he lifted it out, the rotted fabric beneath no longer able to bear their weight. He recognized it immediately, and laid it on the lid of the second case as though it were an artefact from a tomb. He imagined her wearing it, saw the others standing around her, her child's face made impish by her smile and the pointed ears, by her wonderment and excitement at it all. Looking more closely at the inside of the small cap, he found several of her hairs snagged there in the stitching that had once held the sequins in place.

At the inquest, each of the experts called to testify to the tragic consequences of Morgan's final challenge read aloud his or her own list of remarks concerning the inadequacies of his preparations. All demanded to know how the act had been allowed to go ahead in the first place. The Kings, predictably, protested at the unfairness of the questions fired at them in such rapid and destructive salvoes. They were elsewhere surrounded by allies and companions, bound by the lives they led, but here, in the Coroner's Court, they were separated and made to stand alone. They were self-governing, they insisted. They were professionals. It was all too clear to everyone else present that many of their stories had been rehearsed. Explanations fell from excuses like poor grain from blown chaff. They wore the armour of righteous indignation. They were, as ever, their own spectacle, their own sideshow.

But the glare of all these spent stars had long been visible, shedding their heat and light and bulk as they crashed through hostile atmospheres, and now, in this unlikeliest of settings, they flared briefly for the instant before they were extinguished for good.

It pleased Mitchell to see how the journalists of the day had responded to the world they had invaded, how they had entered into the shabby, mocking spirit of the thing, how they had played the game.

There were frequent references in the transcript to the fact that many of the Kings present interrupted the proceedings at every opportunity, and that several of them were evicted from the courtroom – just as they had been evicted from the inquiry into Clarence's death – for shouting obscenities at those passing judgement on Morgan.

Mitchell imagined Quinn among them. There was no mention of him having been called. He and Morgan had remained apart for the previous two years. Perhaps he had attended in the hope of seeing the girl, but had not found her there.

44

So, murder number four. What did she have to offer that might fit the picture, might help the pattern to take shape?

These are glib, predictable thoughts, but convenient. The readers of the newspaper all speak the same language, they all see the same pictures through the same frame of mind.

A man walking his dog. And it sometimes seems to the police as though every crime in the country concerning the discovery of a murdered woman's body involves a man walking his dog.

More stakes and tape. More proof, if proof were needed, that a stolid constable with his hands held behind his back and staring implacably into the middle distance was the true force of the law.

Someone thought they might have heard something. The overgrown dunes were the haunt of courting couples.

A shot of the distant sea and town, the line of hotels crowning the slope running away from the foreground undergrowth. Good light in the sea air. Another picture of the footprints leading in to where the body was found. Here and there an individual trail, but overall a tangled filigree of prints where before and after have become confused.

Questions about the weather, the direction of the wind, the reach of the tide, the sifting of the fine sand.

He studies the photograph another man – one of his rivals now – has taken. She looks like someone caught dancing, only flattened, her arms and legs frozen and then laid down as she spun in her partner's arms. It is a picture he would have been pleased to have taken. The man was local to the south-west. He must have arrived there before the police had organized themselves. Flattened and then laid down. The blood from her throat and slashed stomach and chest has bled in silhouette into the sand.

Nice girl, ordinary girl, decent girl. The kind, outraged reader, that you yourself might have known. A father, a mother, a sister and a fiancé drown in the nation's tears.

Everyone hears the squeal of brakes and the slamming of car doors in the night, everyone hears the argument and the noise that might or might not have been a scream, but no-one ever gets to the window in time to see.

He returns home. He draws a line joining the locations at which each of the bodies has been found. Perhaps a perfect square will be revealed and they will have a better idea who to look for. A mosaic has spread across his own wall. Pictures occasionally fall to the floor in the draught from his door and settle on the other bodies there.

He has already had a dozen girlfriends in his young life, and there was not a single one of them in whom he did not search for and find some unforgettable part of his own dead sister.

He wants another photograph of the man they are holding taken at a time before all this started. He knows the age of the man. He wants a picture of him taken when he was his own age now.

45

This time when she turned to face him she saw that instead of merely going through the motions with the swords, Mitchell seemed to be gaining some genuine pleasure from his performance. It was how he'd been when they first started working together. She listened to everything he said. She wondered if he'd had too much to drink, but then dismissed the idea. There had been times in the past when he'd had difficulty locating the sword slits, no larger than the edges of coins, and when the audience had laughed at him for this. On one occasion, a private party, someone had thrown a piece of cooked chicken at him and he had picked it up off the stage and eaten it before throwing the bones back.

Mitchell himself had never stood inside the cabinet

and worked the levers while she took his place outside. She had once thought they were the two inseparable halves of the single act, but was soon disabused of this. She saw all the publicity photographs of Mitchell with his previous assistants.

Then she tried to remember how much she had had to drink through that cold afternoon and night. She reassured herself by quickly considering everything she had yet to do. She recited the list of codewords and their meanings Mitchell had yet to use. Although she could not explain it, she resented the satisfaction Mitchell now seemed to be getting from the act.

He came closer to the cabinet with sword two, the blade that would pass through her stomach from front to back, after which he would half turn the cabinet, reveal the tip and then turn the cabinet back. She saw the flash of silver in the light and then felt a jolt as he pushed the blade into its slot with more force than was necessary. She steadied herself, one palm flat against the side, ensuring that the tip emerged perfectly timed.

The cabinet stopped shaking. She looked to the side of the stage and watched as the beauty contestants turned and left. That's right, she thought. This isn't what you want to see, so don't look. Tell yourselves that this is not what you are going to end up doing in a million years.

46

Quinn grew suddenly tired of the tale he was having
such difficulty in telling. Something about it no longer
satisfied him. It occurred to Mitchell that the old man
had expected it to be a greater release than it had proved.
Something had been crippled by its containment, and
even released, the story could do nothing more than
stumble forwards and fall. The past had neither turned
into the satisfying substance of history, nor had it
endorsed the present. There was now something pathetic
in the stories Quinn told, in the feelings he continued to
suppress. Something pathetic, too, though perhaps less
definable, in the way these memories had grown ragged
around him, as disappointing to him now as an uncaring
child or a bad investment.

'Good liars,' he said, leaving Mitchell uncertain whether he was speaking for himself or merely repeating something else he had been told, 'jump into the deepest pools of deception, whereas the best a poor liar can do is to kick his feet around in the shallows, always within easy reach of the shore and ready to run splashing back there at the first sign of trouble.'

Mitchell knew it was Arbuckle talking. It seemed a credible enough memory, merely diluted now by time and its constant retelling.

'There's a bottle in the kitchen if you're interested,' Quinn said, meaning for Mitchell to fetch it in to them.

Mitchell went for it. He took two glasses from a pile of unwashed crockery and rinsed them out. He considered pouring himself a drink before returning to Quinn, but then saw the old man watching him in the mirror.

When he returned, Quinn was holding out a news-paper article. At first Mitchell thought this might be something connected to Morgan, but as he exchanged it for the bottle and Quinn poured them both drinks, he saw that it was an article about the recent discovery in America of Cecil B. de Mille's long-lost set for *The Ten Commandments*.

'A hundred miles outside of the city. He built it all. I worked on it with Morgan. Ten storeys high, some of those buildings. Pyramids built in the background a hundred feet high. They made the film, big success, and then someone worked out that it would be too costly to dismantle the thing and so they left it where it was.'

So?

'I worked on the moulds, helped build the Sphinx. Morgan was on a crew of carpenters. I was still only a kid.'

And?

'They only found it again because all the sand that buried it in a sandstorm took another seventy years to blow away again. I stayed for the filming, but Morgan was long gone by then, off with his new film friends. I wanted nothing to do with it.'

He paused to drink, motioning for Mitchell to do the same. The whisky was cheap and raw, with a chemical aftertaste.

'You've had better,' Quinn said, and Mitchell was too slow in answering to sound convincing. 'Ask me, de Mille left it there for a big joke. He was an intellectual. He saw what was happening, even then, he knew what he was surrounded by. So he left it to get buried there, knowing that a long time after he was dead it would all turn up again, this long-lost civilization. According to that—' he pointed his glass at the article in Mitchell's hand, and which Mitchell only pretended to read '—there are those who insist it's real. Two and a half thousand people lived in that place, three hundred animals, camels, elephants, even giraffes. They killed thirty horses and two men, volunteer soldiers, in the filming, chariot race.'

Mitchell put the article on the floor beside him.

'You were never fully convinced one way or the other, were you?' he said.

Quinn pretended not to understand him.

'One word from you, an address, a hiding place, and the police would have known for certain whether or not Morgan was involved in any of the killings.'

'There were too many other considerations.'

'I know,' Mitchell said. And that, above all else, and despite all your protestations to the contrary, is why you too continue to inhabit the waste of the past and wander there in ever-decreasing circles.

47

Clippings have been carefully cut out and pasted. The photographer is pleased with the result. He knows something is missing, knows something has started the slow, downward trail to its unsatisfactory conclusion.

The man has been held for four days. Nothing definite or damning has been discovered, no confession breathed. The other photographers and reporters are losing interest. The facts of the case are turning to ash; someone ham-fisted is excavating the site; more is being lost or destroyed than discovered.

The photographer – Our Photographer, Our Man At The Scene, Our Man In The Know – understands this as well as any of them. The time has come for a retreat into the imagination. He has plotted the route well, knows precisely which narrow and tortuous alleyways will lead him to the man at the table before he is lost to them all.

Pictures of women. Living women, dead women, a wedding album, a baby book, a scatter of almost-known and anonymous faces, carefully written autographs, those same curling fingers, that same white, stiletto-heeled shoe hanging ready to drop from a stiffening foot.

Elsewhere, although all of this the photographer hears and sees, knowing exactly when to look from one man to another, mouthing the words in anticipation of the speakers:

Right, let's begin again, shall we?

If you say so.

I do say so. Oh, I say so, all right.

Right.

The detective by the door, away from the table and its connections, coughs and raises a hand to his mouth. In the corner, the silent stenographer continues to pan every seeming irrelevance for its glint of guilt.

The facts are these: on or around the eighteenth of October last you did assault and kill Doreen Marjorie Brownell at or in the vicinity of—

Everything is lost in the language, in the even strides of the procedure. The senior detective regrets this. Morgan senses it.

And which one was she?

Let him finish.

Not the honey-, the straw- or the platinum-blonde.

Not a particularly clear photograph. Not a photograph a professional news photographer of today might be proud to have taken.

Seventeen lash marks on her face and even more on her partially undressed body. Sexually assaulted before death, and, in all likelihood, afterwards too.

In the photograph one of her arms is wrapped with long grass and the trailing vines of ivy torn from a tree. She became tangled in these as she was pushed or rolled down the short bank. There was some suggestion initially that they might have grown around her after her death, but she was too short a time dead for that.

Another empty site, derelict since the war. It may be a pattern, but it is the pattern of endless, evenly spaced black dots on a plain of white.

Doreen Marjorie Brownell had spent the previous evening drinking at the Panama Club in Mayfair.

That's the Panama Club. Mayfair. Do you know it?

Never heard of it.

Only it's not unlike, not totally dissimilar to the club in which that other young woman, the one you admit to having met, the young woman whose scarf you stole, in which she was last seen alive with you, which she and you were seen to leave together, and after which— (That might be the end of the sentence; it might be left open; there might be more to say.)

Of all his collection of photographs, this is the one in which the woman, though dead, looks most alive, as though, having once been so full of life, some of its warmth is still radiating from her, as though something belonging to life remains, and from which she might, impossibly, begin anew.

48

Three months ago, the end of September, when even the weekends were falling off and the wet cloth of summer was finally wrung dry, Mitchell had gone to see a solicitor. He had travelled thirty miles to see the man, far enough to sever all connections with the town. He told Laura about it only afterwards. He had wanted to know where he stood.

'To feel the ground beneath your knees,' Laura had said.

He had been honest with the man about his mismanagement and his losses, but he had not been honest about his dishonesties. He had taken a case of documents with him. He had gone to the man's office on the fifteenth floor of a new tower block, rising up the outside of the building in a glass lift. He had ascended alone, enjoying the view of the city as it was revealed beneath him like a spreading pool of water. He looked in what he believed was the direction of the coast, grateful, even at that height, that nothing of it was visible.

The solicitor had studied the conditions of his lease and the figures Mitchell showed him. He explained how Mitchell might cushion the blows, how the sharper points might be blunted. It was the solicitor who advised Mitchell to keep away from the courts, who had not advised him against throwing dirt. He had said it was the coward's way out, but that Mitchell was a coward anyway, so it was an appropriate response. Mitchell had repeated that to Laura, too, and she had agreed with the solicitor. They planned the first of their strategies. Autumn was coming, summer was prised away and out of reach. They had plenty of time.

She remembered all this as sword six approached its slot. There was already the start of a cramp in her upper arms. She peered out. Everything she had seen before, she saw again.

She timed the sword through her muscle and flesh and triggered switch six. There were thirteen swords, and that had been Mitchell's idea.

Beneath her, in the glow of the lights from the stage, she could see that the wealthy widow was whispering into the mayor's ear. Both she and the man burst into laughter at the same instant. When the world finally ended, Laura thought, this was how it would end, and all these details would be the minutiae of that explosion.

49

The recommendations of the inquest bled through pages of hairline print into legislation. Reckless bravado was translated into the foreign language of seat belts, restraining bars, safety nets and empty cages.

The details of Morgan's preparations became of secondary importance, too obvious to bear constant repetition: insufficient understanding of the function of the double mould and the interplay of its strengths and weaknesses; of the cooling, consolidation and expansion rates of crushed ice; of the need for speed; of the function of the concealed rods in preventing the ice and water from forming into a single crushing mass. An endless list. One giant detail spawning a thousand others.

But surely nothing here that Morgan himself would

not have considered as the first of the ice hit his shoulders, as its chilling mash ran over him.

It was this conviction – that Morgan alone understood the hidden truths of what was happening – that caused Mitchell to turn from the man to his mother, and to begin the equally unsuccessful assault on the ramparts of the silence behind which she herself had long since withdrawn in the hope that no-one would afterwards come in search of her.

In the solitary photograph he possessed of her taken at that time, she was a slight, dark, attractive girl, one of millions.

50 _____

Oh, the man thinks, as another might say the word, Oh, just the texture, the feel, the colour, the strength and the give of such unyielding flesh. The tightness of her underclothes, the shading of her stockings, the imprints left on her white flesh, the ripple of her body as she fell, and that all-seeing blindness in her eyes as he started. Was that before or after? It hardly mattered then, and it hardly mattered now to remember, except that pleasure and excitement were distilled in all these things. They can search as long as they like, but they will never see what he saw then and what he sees still.

He wakes early in the cold mornings, the collapse of the night into those hours between two and five where neither the day past nor the day coming seems of any consequence, and where a vacuum exists waiting only to be filled. He will soon need to move to somewhere larger, to take everything down from his walls, gather everything up from the floor and pack it away, like those earlier pictures carefully folded between tissue.

She had begged him in one of those dark spaces, yes, *begged* – but how can he ever suggest such a thing? – *begged* him, and even when she had known what must happen to her, she had gone on begging him, begging him because the world must not stop, and because her abandonment, this once as never before and never again, must not now be denied, must be forever complete and unregretted.

And he can see and know and remember all that in the shapes of his imagination and the shading of his pictures. He can even take a photograph of himself studying himself, looking over all these other pictures.

He has already arranged with his journalist companion to visit that one place where he knows something everyone else has overlooked awaits discovery.

He has spoken to other photographers in the better clubs and bars he now frequents and has found a man who, several years earlier, surreptitiously photographed the hanging of a man in Pentonville, convicted of murdering two women. But they had been his greedy girlfriend and unforgiving wife, and so the drama then had been contained and disappointingly predictable within its girdle of tawdry facts.

A photograph of the praying padre, his finger in the

pages of a bible as though, like a bird sucking nectar, he was drawing some sustenance from it.

A picture of the prison clock at the moment the bolt was slid.

A picture of the posting of the notice outside.

A picture of the sandbags, not required on the day, but brought by the hangman just in case.

A picture of the prison cemetery where the headstones were crowded together, as though for cold comfort and forgiveness, no pretence that the plots beneath them were the length of a man.

He is distracted by these thoughts. Another self-portrait. And he is blinded by the light for which he has not prepared himself, knowing even as he half turns and half raises his hand that when the photograph is developed he will be caught with that imbecilic grin, his gestures blurred and uncontrolled, and staring vacantly towards the lens as though there were nothing to see for a thousand miles beyond it.

A picture of the hooded man already counting backwards to infinity.

51

Mitchell first met Laura after talking to a man who told him he was having an affair with a woman twenty years younger than himself, who called herself an actress, or a singer, or a dancer, or a model, and who was currently spending her time dressed as a mermaid and sitting alongside a tank of sharks to help promote the recently opened London Aquarium. He was a married man with two young children, and by the way he spoke Mitchell knew he would forget the woman at the first dry swallow of guilt. He described in great detail how she looked, emphasizing her youth to flatter himself, every detail of her mermaid's costume and her long blond wig and the way she sat on a fibreglass rock, flapped her tail and handed out leaflets to everyone entering the dark space behind her. He said she'd been wearing the bottom half of her costume the first time they'd made love, her tail pulled off only at the last, uncontrollable moment.

Mitchell had gone to the aquarium one Sunday morning. The woman was just as the man had described her. The new attraction was not open for a further hour. The mermaid sat on a bench and smoked three cigarettes in succession. Mitchell approached her and asked for a light. He made no reference to how she was dressed. Eventually, she screwed out her third cigarette and searched for the non-existent fourth in her packet. She swore and Mitchell offered her one of his own.

His first words to her were to remark that she did not strike him as a particularly happy mermaid. She told him she had a hangover. There was a problem with the tank which an engineer was fixing. She wanted to be inside, sitting in the gloom. The sun hurt her eyes. She asked him what he was doing there, and when he said he was interested in sharks, she looked him up and down and laughed at him. He asked her if she wanted to go for a drink with him. It was ten o'clock. 'Nowhere open,' she said. 'And besides . . .' She indicated the poster showing the sharks over her shoulder. He asked her how she'd got the job.

'Silver tail on a leotard, wig, glitter on my cheeks, cockle shells on my—' She shaped her hands over her breasts. 'How do you think I got it? I beat hundreds of other applicants at an audition for it. Cinderella job. I was the first one to get into the tail.'

He asked her if the sharks were worth seeing and she shrugged. She called them fish and said they were ugly. She'd been sent outside to smoke while the tank was being fixed. Her flimsy smile appealed to Mitchell. She said the aquarium manager had made a point of telling her not to let the public see her smoking. A smoking mermaid was not good for business.

Mitchell told her he wanted to see the sharks and she flicked her tail at him and laughed.

52

Criminal incompetence and negligence. Hammer blows to the Kings still reeling from Morgan's death. The inquest lasted four days, twice as long as expected. From the front page to pages further and further back. Blow after blow after blow. Several of the minor Kings followed his mother's example and disappeared. A constellation of slapstick stars was dying in the distant corner of a makeshift galaxy, and the only people who cared enough to look up and watch hadn't the faintest idea what they were seeing.

'Final Act,' the press announced. 'The Curtain Fails', 'Trouper's Tragedy', 'Ice Tomb'.

Blow after blow after blow. And the chocks were knocked aside and the once-mighty vessel of the Kings dragged its chains down the slipway and continued unstoppable to the bottom of the river.

A dynasty had ended messily, like most.

Incredulity, pity and contempt were never any defence, never a buttress against what was to come. There remained too much faith in the quest for fickle celebrity.

The human cannonball flew through the air and fell to the ground.

Some of them persevered, of course, those who had stared too long into the sun of fame and been blinded by it, but after Morgan, watching them had been like looking through a sheet of plate glass which was shattered but still intact and ready to fall apart at the exposure of the slightest illusion. Audiences no longer fooled themselves. The snake-charmer blew and blew and the only hissing now came from the watching crowd.

53

Eight years ago, a previous manager had hanged himself in one of the club's storerooms, undiscovered for four days, during which time, the second week in January, no-one had missed him, his body finally being discovered by an electrician called in to discover why most of the ceiling lights in the ballroom had suddenly fused.

No-one was any longer certain of which of the several storerooms the man had chosen. There was even a suggestion that it might have been the dressing room, the one in which the beauty contestants now waited, and which had previously been used as a store. The tale, as all the tales around it, was endlessly accommodating, spinning one way and then the other as all its vital tensions were released.

A man at the bar – the full length of which was visible to Laura through the panel in the cabinet door – fitted a dozen drinks on to a tin tray and moved among the judges' tables. She saw several of the dancers among the crowd.

A tap for sword seven.

What are you thinking about?

Nothing.

The approaching blade. In one side of – *one* – her waist – *two* – and out the – *three* – other.

54

He sits and watches his face speeding over the flat land-scape, brought vividly to life as the train passes through the tunnel, every feature, every line cast into sharp relief. He sees the others watching themselves pass through the darkness, and only then does it occur to him that this is the same way that the other man must have come. He has searched the newspapers, but found nothing new.

At Clacton, he and the reporter take a taxi. He gives the driver the address he has been given, the address for which he has paid good money. Neither man betrays their mission.

It is a satisfyingly run-down street. Grey cement stucco is peeling in slabs from the front of the house. Grass grows in the high gutters. The lace curtains at two of the windows are lifted and dropped. They press a succession of bells. He takes a photograph of the nameplates. Nothing there except the waiting spaces into which speculation might later flood.

Other theatricals. The man at the police station is well known to them, of course he is, of course. Most are eager to talk, all awaiting their own small part in the drama. No, no-one from the police has been there yet. They assumed everything was happening in London or Southend. They are undecided as to the man's guilt. Some proclaim his innocence as loudly as he himself must now be doing; others indulge themselves in the shadow-play of doubt. The interviewees are reduced to four. A drink is suggested. Would it be possible to take a few photographs? Background, general stuff, nothing specific, no faces, if that was what they wanted.

What did he want to see?

He is about to suggest whatever they want to show him when one of them suggests the girl.

The girl?

What will happen to her? another asks.

The reporter takes out his notebook and cautiously asks the first of his questions. Some respond as though he had taken out a pistol and was now pointing it at them. Others become more enthusiastic.

Six of them climb the stairs to the second floor.

A door is pointed out.

Flash.

One of them knocks.

No answer.

'We're friends of Morgan King,' the photographer calls out.

They hear movement inside.

A bolt is drawn, a catch turned. A voice. A woman talking softly to a child.

The photographer stands back, his camera held ready. He motions for the others to clear a space around the door.

'Ready?' the reporter whispers to him.

55

What more can I tell you? the man at the table seems to say. What is there that you don't already know? What is there that you will never know?

The senior detective has already given up the chase. Procedure and protocol are all that remain. He knows it is a common enough trick, too complicated for many, to give as much as possible while withholding the vital piece of information. The closer a suspect brings himself to the place and time and manner of the crime, the more credible he believes he becomes. But there is still not enough to prosecute. Too many inconsistencies and contradictions when all the killings are viewed together. And there is too much public interest now, too many articles and pictures, to make a mistake and not lose face. He wonders how long it will be before his own lack of conviction is sensed by the two junior detectives, and how soon after that they themselves will give the game away. There have already been long periods recently in the interview when he has signalled to the stenographer to rest his fingers. He does it again now at the mention of the train.

'We entered the tunnel at such a slow speed. Work was being carried out on the track, and in the darkness the train slowed even further. You could walk faster.'

No-one hurries him, no-one urges him to get to the point, and for this the man at the table appears grateful. He is already imagining his walk out into the daylight, already preparing to capitalize on what he has allowed himself to become.

'And at regular intervals along the tunnel there were recesses set into the curved brick wall, and in each of these there was a man, standing upright and with his arms pressed to his sides just like the statue of a saint in its niche in a church, all of them just standing there, inches away from us and watching us go past.'

He loses himself in the reminiscence, unaware of the silence spreading from the corner of the room.

He has known for the past hour that he will soon be leaving, that the game is over, and he is already imagining the reception that awaits him, the reception outside, on the steps, in the street, and then further away and further, the reception that awaits him in all the places he has yet to appear and perform. And just as he imagines all this and his own overblown speech of release, so he also tries to imagine where precisely in that autumn morning sky the cold sun will be and how brightly it will be shining down on him, how dark and long his outline might fall behind him as his guilt is shed.

It was said of the most famous of the Kings that ordinary people would pay good money just to stand in their shadows.

When he was a boy, before he was abandoned and before he went to America, he used to stand in those same shallow recesses in a tunnel near his home, take a deep breath at the thunderous approach of the train and then feel giddy and exhilarated as the passing engine sucked out all the air and filled the tunnel instead with its steam and smoke. He would emerge blackened from head to foot, a different person entirely, a creature of a boy, a taste in his mouth he had never tasted before and seldom tasted since.

56

Down at the mayor's table, the mayor and his friends rose at the approach of his granddaughter. The beautiful girl hugged him and kissed him. The other men straightened their ties and pushed back their hair with their fingers as though she might be about to bestow the same favour on them. Only the wealthy widow remained in her seat. The mayor introduced the girl to the others. Two of the men took her hand and kissed it. The girl acted flattered in front of her grandfather. Everyone except the wealthy widow offered to buy her a drink. They shuffled the chairs round the table to make room for her, all of them hoping she would sit beside them. The girl wore her coat, clutching it at her chest, hiding her beautiful body beneath. Her hair, her lips and her eyes shone in the light.

Laura saw all this. She watched the girl, but mostly she watched the wealthy widow. No-one at the table paid any attention to Mitchell or his cabinet on the stage, and she knew that she, Laura, had already ceased to exist as far as most of the audience were concerned.

Down at the table, the girl refused all entreaties for her to remove her coat. Only the wealthy widow said nothing. She lifted her hand to attract one of the waitresses and her jewellery blazed at her wrist. It was clear to everyone who spoke to her that the woman already regretted having come home from Spain, and that she would return to the warmth and the other brown, wealthy widows there at the earliest opportunity.

Sword eight. In left lower chest. Out right upper.

Sword nine. In dead centre front. Out dead centre back.

Sword ten. In left ear. Out right ear.

Perfect symmetry, this pattern of destruction.

Laura rubbed her eyes, a difficult manoeuvre within the confines of the box.

She wondered if Mitchell was now intent on giving the twenty-minute show, or if, for some unfathomable reason known only to him, he had decided to prolong it even further.

She no longer listened to what he was saying. Everything he said she had already heard a hundred times before.

She sensed the clock of the old year winding down, ticking slower and slower to the silence of its end.

57

There were over five hundred present at Morgan's funeral, and as many again held back at the gates. The Kings were all gathered, the drawstring pulled tight across half a continent, and here they all were. Most of the faces of those standing closest to the grave were poorly defined and lost further in enlargement. Mitchell had made a note of the few he was able to identify. There was Morgan's brother, three of his cousins, and a cousin of his own, a woman twenty-six years older than himself. No sign of Quinn or of his mother. Further back the groups of figures merge into a single mass, men and women, old and young, Kings and onlookers, those there to grieve, and those there to watch simply because it had always been their right to watch and they would not be denied this valedictory performance now.

It was reported that three detectives had attended, but finding them in the picture was impossible. The best Mitchell could do was pick out a group of men standing together and at a short distance from the others. But these might just as easily have been the undertaker's employees, or gravediggers, or drivers stamping their feet in the cold.

The reports concerning the number of wreaths seemed true – mounds of them spilling around the grave and covering nearby plots. It did not require too much effort to guess their colours or to see the final acts of showmanship that had gone into those opulent hearts and stars and giant letter *M*s.

After that, the Kings again dispersed, their stories corroborated, speculations harvested, myths planted, and the end came to them like the long hard winter that was already forecast – a few more exploratory jabs of the blade under cover of night, and then the long sure drive to their exposed and waiting hearts. And when it came they fell like the melodramatic Priams, Lears and Macbeths they were, clutching at their chests and wasting their own dying words shouting in surprised, aggrieved tones of their innocence and their betrayal, of being deceived by the times which had nurtured them and then thrown them down and trampled on them.

It pleased Mitchell to sustain these metaphors. He did not pretend he was breathing the breath of new life into them – some of them were embarrassingly unavoidable – but nor could he deny that he had used them to maintain a distance and to shield himself from all the bloody and undeniable details of all he had not yet seen and might never see. It was not a strong shield – nowhere near as strong as his mother's silence had been during all those years afterwards – but it served its purpose, and like that curtain drawn across the stage, it kept the two halves of the one small world inviolate and apart.

58

'I know I should have done more for her. Perhaps I should have taken her out of that place by force and brought her here. Waited until all the interest died down and done something about it.'

'But Morgan was released and *he* went and got her instead.'

'Got her and left the same day. He wrote telling me where to send everything.'

'Did you try to get in touch with either of them?'

'A few times. Once. About six months later. I met someone who'd seen Morgan in Manchester. He knew what Morgan was planning – the ice cabinet – and told me about it. I asked him about your mother, but the man hadn't seen her. Morgan told him she was still with him, that she was helping him prepare the act.'

'And the next thing you knew—'

'Was that he'd gone ahead with it and failed, and that your mother—'

'That she'd gone.'

'The murders went on. The police went back to see him, but it soon became obvious that he couldn't have been responsible.'

'Not even for the ones they arrested him in connection with?'

It only then occurred to Mitchell that the nightclub blonde had been killed all those years ago less than fifteen minutes' walk from where they now sat in the sinking summer's day.

Quinn refused to answer. He raised his glass to his mouth, but it was empty. 'What do I know?'

'You knew what he was capable of.'

'Did I? I dug this out for you. You probably never saw it.' He handed Mitchell yet another newspaper clipping. The edges of the story were fraying and yellowing in every direction.

The woman stood at her open door, one hand held forward, the other clasping the edge of the frame. She has been surprised by the flash of the camera, that much is clear. Behind her, the light from a window shows something of a room. Mitchell read the short article beneath, which told him nothing except the woman's name and that she denied all knowledge of Morgan and what he might or might not have done.

'Another so-called witness?' Mitchell said.

'Not really.'

'Whatever, it's not much of a conclusion.'

'Look behind her,' Quinn said.

Mitchell looked more closely and saw the small figure, a girl, her features barely distinguishable in the poor print, badly lit, sitting on the edge of a bed or a sofa, her feet hardly reaching the floor.

'It's her,' Quinn said.

The woman at the door was shouting to make herself heard above the insistent voices of the photographer and the journalist, both of whom were holding the door open against her pushing.

59 _____

A longer pause than usual between the swords.

She waited. Thinking about her life ahead, about her life without Mitchell, about leaving the town and finding another like it and starting again. Nothing that mattered ever changed; only the superficial and disposable details of the process changed.

The previous night she had watched the waves rise above the Promenade wall. The snow had been forecast for then, but had come a day late. She had watched the outlines of the hovering gulls like ghosts in the darkness. There had been no illuminations, only the glow of the lights along the seafront, sole markers of where the land ended and the water began. She had wondered then, and not for the first time, what brought her to these places and what kept her at ease with the limitless darkness into which she and a million others like her might so easily disappear.

60 _____

The Panama Club, in Mayfair, has palm trees and pink flamingos on the walls. The photographer touches one of the birds and feels it sway on its hook.

The manufacturer of pink flamingos and palm trees and musical notes and black cats for the decoration of the club walls must have become a millionaire that year.

Not for the first time in his life, the photographer imagines himself to be invisible.

The Panama Club, or so his colleague has written, was known to be the haunt of men like himself and of women like the woman sitting beside him. She disturbs his thoughts by asking him if this is his first time there. She hasn't seen him there before. She would have remembered. She moved closer to him. Funny he should have come in on *that* night of all nights. She herself hadn't been well. This was her first time out in a fortnight. She needed spoiling. Would he like to spoil her? She lived near by. Pampering, that was the word. She played with the fake pearls of her necklace, letting her fingers rest briefly in her cleavage, letting him look. Did he want to dance? Some did, some didn't; she always asked. No, he didn't dance. A drink, then? Pink champagne or something even more exotic? She hoped he wasn't going to disappoint her by leaving her alone. No, he said, he wasn't going to leave her alone. He asked her her name. He showed her his card which said he was a professional photographer. She became more interested in him. She told him her name and he told her he had known someone else called the same. Small world, she said. She sat so that her leg pressed against his along its full length. She wasn't much of a dancer herself. She would be happy just to sit and talk. He did understand the rules, didn't he? If it was up to her— Their drinks arrived. What sort of photographer? Fashion, society, crime, magazines, what? Yes, he told her, all of that.

61

The room let in no natural light and the tank at its centre was illuminated by four rows of spotlights, some shining up from a low rail, others casting their light from the overhead rig. The pale undersides of the sharks showed occasionally through the gloom as they came close to the glass and then flicked away from it at the last moment, their eyes and teeth glimpsed only for an instant. The water in the tank was green and opaque and filled with coarse sediment in suspension. Small pieces of white meat drifted in this and were seized by the sharks. A thin slime already coated the inside of the glass along its lower edges where pebbles and sand had been poured.

Mitchell stood beside the mermaid on her rock. She sat with her back to the tank, looking out into the main entrance and the distant daylight there. She gave a leaflet to everyone who passed her on their way to the sharks.

A man with two small children returned from his circuit of the giant tank to complain about how little they had seen, how disappointed his daughters were.

'I can't make them come and look out at you,' the mermaid told him.

Mitchell moved away from her, closer to the glass.

The creatures inside moved effortlessly to and fro, like half-remembered shapes in a nightmare. Other men waited with cameras.

He returned to the mermaid. The disappointed man and his children remained beside her. She asked him what he wanted her to do. He asked her for a refund. She was about to answer him when she half turned to Mitchell, pointed over his shoulder and said 'Look,' and he turned just in time to see a hammerhead shark collide with the glass, bare the tooth-filled underside of its tube-shaped head and then turn upwards so that the pearly grey of its belly was pressed against the glass as it rose to the surface. Mitchell had never seen anything so ugly, or so threatening in its ugliness, so close before. He waited for the creature to reappear, but it never came.

'There,' the mermaid said to the disappointed customer, but the man was distracted by the sudden crying of one of his daughters who wept convulsively and who stood pointing to where the shark had so suddenly appeared and then gone. Unable to calm her where she stood, the man picked her up and carried her away.

'Another satisfied customer,' the mermaid said to Mitchell.

He smiled and asked her name.

'Laura,' she said. 'Little mermaid Laura.'

'Shark woman,' he said. He asked her how long she expected the job to last.

She looked at her watch and flicked her tail.

62

'You were there, weren't you?' Mitchell said.

There where? But he didn't say it. 'It's all you ever wanted to know of me.'

'Blackpool. You saw everything.'

'Thirty-first of October, 1926.'

'What?'

'Day Harry Houdini died.'

'So?'

'The exact same day Morgan walked out on me to star in the first of his films. Funny how all of those connections exist, that all you have to do is look for them.'

'There must have been others there, other Kings.'

'Oh, they were there, all right.'

'But none of them recognized you?'

'I grew a beard, wore glasses, it doesn't matter. I was there and none of them recognized me. You don't know how good that felt. I never forgot how many of them turned out for Morgan's funeral, and how few of them – how *none* of them – turned up at the small service that was held for my brother, killed fighting for his King and Country.'

'You could have stopped everything happening.'

'Stopped what? I could barely stop myself from shaking, being back among them like that. I was on the front row. There were times when she came as close to me then as you are to me now. That close.'

'And even *she* didn't recognize you?'

'I would have loved her and taken care of her for ever.'

'I know you would,' Mitchell said.

'That close.'

'And is this what she wore that night?' He held up the silver-framed photograph which was still in his lap.

'I bought it in the foyer.'

'Were there pictures of the ice cabinet?'

'Of course there were. And of him.'

'Had you gone intending to speak to her?'

'It had been two years.'

'Or were you there just to watch Morgan kill himself?'

'Both, I suppose. I don't know.'

'But that's what you believed he was doing?'

Quinn nodded.

'What? An act of atonement? Suicide? A grand, final gesture?'

'See, even you can't pull the two halves apart.'

'Did you think you were alone in knowing what he was doing?'

'What do you think?'

'And either way, the Kings got their headlines.'

'She danced around him. She sang a song, something she always used to sing. I thought I'd choke to hear it again. She danced around that stage as though she were floating an inch above it.'

The dying planet and its small, spinning moon.

'I barely saw what he was doing. I watched her. Not him, her.'

You wanted him dead and her out of his clutches.

'There was one moment when I— when she— I mean—'

'When she saw you.'

'When she looked directly at me. Only for an instant, a second, less, but she looked straight at me and I thought, I swear to God I thought— but then she looked at someone else and went on singing and dancing without missing a beat.'

'But you think she saw you?'

'Saw me, but that's all.'

'Were you going to tell me any of this?'

Quinn took back the photograph. 'I don't know.'

Mitchell believed him. 'Whatever he was, or did, he would never have harmed her.'

'No.'

'Her life afterwards was nothing by comparison with everything that had already happened.'

'I can imagine. When I heard your father had died I thanked God and wished it had happened sooner.'

And you knew from that instant that one day I'd come to find you.

'All the details, the act, the cabinet, no-one told it afterwards like it was, not even at the inquest,' Quinn said.

'I can imagine.'

'A bloody mess. Nothing gave. Only him. They were smashing away at the glass and the frame for twenty minutes before anything happened. He was a bloody mess. Someone said he looked as though he'd fallen a hundred feet on to concrete. Someone else said they didn't think he'd made the slightest effort to stop the ice from getting to him.'

'And you sat and watched it all happen.'

'I sat and watched it all happen.'

'And afterwards—'

'And afterwards she was gone for ever, running into whatever was left for her.'

'By which time you were convinced that in addition to having killed himself, he'd killed at least one of those women.'

Quinn raised his hands to his face.

'Do you think he knew you were in the audience?'

'I'm certain of it.'

'Oh?'

'There was a panel kept clear of ice. You could see his face.'

'And he saw you?'

'Saw me? I'd swear in a court of law that he was standing there staring out at me for the whole of the hour it took for the ice to freeze around him and then for them to try and smash him out of it.'

Mitchell looked again at the photograph, and the instant his eyes met hers he heard the song she used to sing to him as a child.

He rose after that and told Quinn he was leaving.

The old man took back the photograph of the girl and held it to his chest. He started to cry.

'I know you would have loved her and cared for her,' Mitchell said. But it was consolation to neither of them.

He left the room and waited briefly in the hallway. The sound of Quinn's crying grew louder, coming to him distorted through the wall.

He left the tomb of the house and stood outside in the warmth of the early evening sun. He looked back at the window, relieved to see that Quinn was not standing there and watching him go.

He made his way to where he had parked his car. A small girl ran shouting ahead of him along the street.

63

She moved her foot from pedal ten to pedal eleven and waited.

She had once forgotten her place in the sequence of the swords and Left Breast Upper had come out Right Thigh Lower, giving them their loudest applause of the evening.

Her thumb rested on the small round pad, no larger than a typewriter key.

Like the swords, the false blood they had once used had never looked like real blood. Too thick, too red under the lights. Too much like what people expected to see.

A shout from the audience distracted her. Her first instinct was to press the pad, but she waited.

'Eleven,' she said, more to herself than to Mitchell.

Nothing.

She looked out over the faces below.

The partitions which enclosed her were fastened from the outside. No provision was made for her to release herself from within the cabinet.

The call from the audience was followed by another. She expected to hear Mitchell shout back.

She looked for him. He was no longer standing where he should have been standing. She turned as best she could in the confined space, looking all around her.

'Mitchell?'

She looked down to the front tables. And from there she looked over the scattered crowd to the bar, to the barman who had earlier given Mitchell the bags of money. She heard the stuttering of the electronic tills through the rising noise of the room.

The calls from the audience became louder, more insistent, and even she, hidden, unseen except for her smiling face, perhaps forgotten by some, felt something of the urgency being generated around her.

'Mitchell?'

She looked down to where the mayor had risen from his seat and was making his way through the crowd towards the club entrance, the men around him and at other tables rising in his wake and following him.

The beautiful girl had pulled her coat even tighter around her and now sat frowning, abandoned by all her admirers. Only the wealthy widow remained calm and in her seat, and she alone looked up to Laura on the stage. She held a drink close to her face and turned away from

Laura to study the beautiful girl through the yellow liquid.

Laura saw her smiling. She considered again calling for Mitchell, but his name died in the heartbeat between her throat and her lips.

64

He dances very well for someone who doesn't dance. They are back in their seats, out of breath, a film of sweat on his forehead and over her bare shoulders and arms.

What kind of photographer again? She knows someone at the club who can get a full bottle at a discount. At that club and others like it. Not *that* kind of photographer, she hopes, but with undisguised enthusiasm. Her leg is once more against his, her hand now resting lightly on his thigh. Perhaps he can take some pictures of her. And no, she does not believe he has a sister called Desirée. It isn't even her own real name. Just one she picked out of a magazine. She isn't even certain if she should spell it with one of those French accent things or not. Not that there have been many opportunities so far for her to have to spell it out. None, in fact. And why, she wants to know, after their last dance, do they have to leave so early? What was so important that he had to be up at five o'clock in the morning? What happened at that time in the morning that was so important? For her, sometimes, five in the morning was the end of the night. She expects him to laugh at this, but he remains oblivious to everything she says, concentrating instead on the moisture beginning to form and run between her breasts, where it is cast into prominence by the alternating red and darkness of his vision.

65

The near-naked man in his upright glass coffin. Air and water fighting for control over him, tempting him to one or the other, transfiguring flesh and blood, and waiting for the cold chambers of his heart to fill and to freeze and then for the growing ruby crystals to swell into ever more intricate designs, each of them a far greater miracle than any of the Kings had ever dreamed of.

Ice that will now flatten and then probe his eyes, finger his ears and his mouth before pushing into him, some demented surgeon, a rod for every orifice, until his entire body constitutes a solitary, open, uncontainable wound, his ribs the spars of a ship in a gathering floe, and ice that will push out from within, gather and clot in his veins and his arteries as he awaits the heartbeat of his impossible spring.

And the watching girl in her silver cape and sequinned cap with its emerald ears, running from the theatre into the enveloping darkness of the night, a small and mystical figure as real to Mitchell now as any other starstruck Icarus who once had the spirit and the nerve to rise from that magical world only to fall back crushed and blinded into another world completely, a world where, for ever afterwards, the best she could do was to crawl and to beg for the eyes and the ears of the dull-witted creatures all around her.

66

She rises. He steadies himself against the wall. What is it? Bit unsteady. Not surprising. His eyes are closed against the vision. She too stumbles as she edges out of her seat and around the small table. He picks up her handbag. You forgot this. She tells him again how grateful she is that he has offered to walk her home. You can't be too careful. She'd forget her own head if it wasn't screwed on.

An announcement: 'Ladies and Gentlemen . . .'

A girl wasn't safe. Still, a pity about him having to go to work so early.

He opens his eyes, as though opening them for the first time, and he sees the slender white gloves she has forgotten to pick up. He follows her out of the seat, scooping them into his pocket as he rises to join her. She asks him if he isn't going to leave any money on the table. It's the done thing. He screws the gloves into a ball in his pocket and feels around them for whatever change he might have. He takes this out and spreads it on the table. Very generous. She could tell he was a generous man the moment she set eyes on him. Wasn't she the lucky one? Not like her friend. What friend? Hadn't she told him about her friend? In all the papers. Not her friend, exactly, more an acquaintance. That's it, acquaintance. Similar line of work, you might say. He can smell the drink on her breath. But he doesn't really want to have to listen to her, not now, not so close. They skirt the edge of the small dance floor.

'Ladies and Gentlemen, Introducing . . .'

Above him, a man and a woman walk out on to the low stage.

He keeps his head down. She waves her farewells to several other women she knows. He wishes she wouldn't.

'For Your Entertainment This Evening . . .'

She whispers excitedly to one of these women. The woman searches in her bag for something and hands it over. The two of them kiss. He watches. The woman on the stage comes to the front so that her waist is level with his head.

67

And when it finally occurs to her what has happened, when she finally understands what feeds this sudden, growing urgency all around her, her first impulse is not to bang on the door of the cabinet or to shout out to be released, but to laugh. Or if not to laugh, then to cheer.

She takes her finger off key eleven.

She reaches behind her and slides the one true sword from its socket, carefully pushing the blade until it falls from the box to the stage with a clatter.

And it strikes her then as she waits for either release or abandonment – neither would count for anything: the end would be the end just the same – that this is what Mitchell has always been to her – a trick, an illusion, a deceit; that this is what he has been to everyone who has ever known him. And realizing this, she feels suddenly reassured, secure in the understanding that everything that now happens to her might be considered merely another small and inconsequential part of the one all-encompassing illusion into which she willingly entered sitting on her fibreglass rock beside the sharks.

She watches as the beauty-show contestants return to the side of the stage, as they gather there and begin to speculate on what is happening.

She watches as the mayor's beautiful granddaughter finally rises from her seat beside the wealthy widow and follows uncertainly after her grandfather.

Above her, more lights are switched on.

Someone she does not recognize arrives on the stage beside her and knocks on the door of the cabinet as though he were knocking on the door of a house.

'Are you still in there?' this stranger says.

Her head no longer fills its oval space.

Through a gap in the side of the cabinet she can see where Mitchell's last three swords have fallen into a giant silver arrow, indicating the precise point and direction of his own unnoticed disappearance.

The man who has knocked fumbles with the bolts. He tells her not to panic.

She waits, perfectly calm and silent in the darkness of the box, the illusion intact, men turned hounds, Mitchell turned fox; waits to emerge with a pose and a flourish, already practising the mix of innocence, achievement and disbelief of which her expression will be composed when she finally steps out, when she finally steps out and bows and presents herself to the waiting world anew.